I0545417

Boss With Benefits

by

Lelani Black

Boss With Benefits

The Wild Rose Press, Inc.
PO Box 708
Adams Basin, NY 14410-0708
Visit us at www.thewildrosepress.com

Publishing History
Second Scarlet Rose Edition, 2020
First Scarlet Rose Edition, February 2010
Trade Paperback ISBN 978-1-5092-3398-4

Published in the United States of America

How could he forget his keys?

Jack was glad that his secretary hadn't locked up and left the office yet.

He stopped dead in his tracks.

Standing in his office was a delicious-looking woman who stared straight back at him with a dazzling pair of inky-lashed green eyes that tilted exotically at the corners. Chestnut hair shot with sunlight tumbled in vivid contrast around the blue denim jacket that she wore over a skimpy top.

Jack frowned, noting a vague resemblance to his secretary. Yet…other than sharing similar height and possibly hair color, there was nothing definitive that he could quite pin down. *"Keely?"*

Her mini-skirt hung low on shapely hips and its funky frayed hem rippled against luscious golden thighs. Jack shook his head slowly.

"Definitely *not* my secretary," Jack murmured the comical thought that flashed through his addled brain. This woman might be a cousin, niece, or sister, but *no way* did those legs belong to the quiet office mouse who worked the front desk!

His nostrils flared. The office smelled different, too, like delicate night flowers. *His* secretary didn't wear perfume.

Dedication

For Pete...I didn't last a day as your secretary,
but thank you for all the fringe benefits.

Chapter One

Jack Sloane hated interruptions, so when his secretary plunked a document on his desk while he was in the middle of an important phone call, he turned his impatient blue gaze the opposite direction and focused instead on the world-famous view of Diamond Head just beyond the windows of his office suite.

It was 4:59 p.m. on Aloha Friday and he wanted out. He was done with work. It was time to *play*. Class and luxury his office's wood-paneled walls and espresso leather chairs might be, but he'd been caged there since 5 a.m.

He was hungry, horny, and the sexy voice on the line belonged to a woman he'd been chasing one day shy of two weeks. Dayna—Jack had met her at the hotel's nightclub on the Garden Terrace below. He'd stopped in to see the bartender, a friend of his, and had watched her dance. She had a gorgeous face, a banging hot body, and Jack wanted her there and then.

Jack found out what she and her friends were drinking, and sent over a complimentary round. The waitress made sure to tell the seashell blonde exactly who'd paid for the drinks, pointing at Jack as he lounged next to the bar. The blonde stood up, walked over, and introduced herself.

"Pleasure to meet you, Dayna." Jack had nodded at

her party. "If you make it an early night, give me a call. I'd love to take you somewhere for a late dinner."

She'd dressed classily, wearing a white mini-skirt, black stockings, black sky-scraper heels, and a snug-fitting cropped black jacket whose deep V-neck flaunted the golden swell of her cleavage.

Jack had been casual in black denim jeans and a black T-shirt. He could tell by the hungry gleam in her eyes that she was impressed by his height, muscled arms, broad shoulders, and taut waist.

"We were just about done here," Dayna said. "The girls were heading off to Moose's on Lewers." She'd studied his ragged jeans, then blinked at the large bump in his crotch.

"Sorry." Jack apologized for the way he dressed. "Worked on an A/C unit today, but my place is just a few minutes from here. I'll change," he said, reading the curiosity on her face, for ZuZu's had a dress code, and he'd gotten in wearing jeans.

Dayna had frowned then, and looked less than thrilled. Maintenance guys were obviously not her style. "Uh, maybe some other time," she'd said with a regretful sigh.

"Okay." Jack had shrugged and turned to talk to his bartender friend. Apparently she didn't like being dismissed so easily, and before she left the club she gave him the name of the office where she worked.

She might not have wanted to go out with him that night, but by God she wanted to get into his pants…

"Hey Dayna, Jack Sloane here. How are you?" he asked, ignoring the fax on his desk that his secretary had marked URGENT, with two exclamation points.

"I'm doing well, thank you. How can I help you,

Jack?"

"I've got reservations for two at J's Beef and Reef on Kalakaua Avenue. Come with me."

He heard her gasp, her voice come to life. "*The* J's Beef and Reef on the strip? How? That place is booked weeks in advance!"

Jack smiled. "I have connections—"

A huffy little snort interrupted Jack's train of thought. He swiveled in his chair, his gaze roaming beyond the open door of his office to where his current secretary worked. She'd come as part of the hotel's business office when he'd bought out the owners four months ago.

One look at the black horn-rimmed glasses propped low on her nose and her eyes squinting up at him and he could barely get beyond anything else, including her hair pulled back in a lop-sided twist with a pencil stuck through.

Quiet, near invisible, she kept the office running smooth, didn't care about current office fashions, and had no interest in conversation-unlike his previous secretaries who were too chatty, wore their hems too high, necklines too low and couldn't get their work done, it seemed, whenever he was around.

She sat at her desk in the reception area, her back turned to him as she typed.

He cleared his throat. "Would you mind shutting my door, Keely? Please?"

"Just one second."

Jack had a mind to shut the door himself, but didn't want to put the lovely Dayna on hold. "Sorry about that, Dayna. So, are we on for tonight?"

"Yeah, I guess. Um, can I meet you there?" Dayna

asked, apparently convinced that he didn't have decent wheels.

"Well, I was hoping I could swing by and pick you up—"

His secretary's muffled laugh once again threw him off.

"Will you excuse me just a sec?" Jack glared at his secretary's back in her mousehair-or was it *mohair-*sweater?

Well, he thought, his irritation softening, she'd heard and seen much worse coming from his office, truth be told, so if this conversation gave her some amusement, then she could listen till the cows came home. Or, she could shut his office door, like he'd asked so nicely earlier.

"Jack, I'd rather we met at the restaurant. Oh, and if we decide to go anywhere afterwards, we can just take my car," Dayna offered.

"Sure, but I had hoped to take you for a moonlit drive along the coast in my roadster. Topless," he replied.

"Topless?"

"The *car*, honey…"

"Oh my," she said, intrigued, and gave him her address. "I'll be downstairs in an hour. Don't be late."

Jack's small smile turned cool as he registered her warning. "I'll be there-"

The sound of his office door being slammed shut turned his wry smile back into a full-fledged grin.

Keely St. John stomped back to her desk and wanted to scream. She could write this headline in her sleep: Mr. Player Reels in a Bimbo.

"Mr. Jack-ass Sloane has done it again," she

mumbled, stabbed the button on the monitor and shut off her computer, never mind exiting out of any word windows.

She'd like to toss him out the window and watch him dive five floors down into the blue lagoon-like swimming pool below, come to think of it. Jack's bimbo-zillas called the office at all hours of the day and condescended to her—Mr. Jack Sloane's mousy doesn't-have-a-life secretary.

Guess she couldn't blame them. That's what she led him, and everyone else, to believe.

The problem was, she didn't have a life. At least, not one that included a good man complete with hot, happy sex. Real sex. Not that she'd been having any fake sex, but she was getting tired of the fantasies starring Jack Sloane. Pipe dreams-that was all they would ever be.

She could not get out often enough to meet a nice man. Working for Jack Sloane and seeing firsthand his playboy antics turned her off to rich, gorgeous bachelors.

Yet, one of his random smiles, his deep voice greeting her with a polite "hello" when he walked into the office, turned her right back on. Hearing his laugh when he was on the phone, even seeing his sexy mouth frown at reports, was enough to send her into a fit of agonized wanting, squirming in her seat throughout the day as her pussy swelled with lust.

She sat back down at her desk, shoulders slumped and heart thumping in her chest. "What is wrong with me?" she fretted.

She needed to quit. Working for her blue-eyed boss was giving her way too much heartburn. Still…while he might be a knucklehead when it came to dating women, he paid her very well. Besides, decent jobs were so hard to come by these days.

Of course, as owner of the Island Lily Hotel, with its salmon-colored stucco and red tile roof situated on the shores of Hawaii's Waikiki beach, Jack Sloane could afford to pay all of his employees great salaries.

Guests paid pretty on their red, gold, and platinum cards to escape to luxurious rooms that looked out over powder-soft sands and a velvet blue ocean. And, working for Jack Sloane helped pay the mortgage on her little ivy-covered cottage in the hibiscus dappled heights of pricey Makiki.

So, if she had to put up with his handsome face, corded muscles, and tight butt, not to mention his snooty girlfriends calling, dropping by, or hanging up on her, surely it was a small price to pay?

She could do without the crash course in Player 101—as if her ex-husband hadn't taught her plenty when he left her for a centerfold. Not just any centerfold either, her ex had tactlessly explained, but a centerfold of the year.

Keely sighed and walked through the large suites, turning off lights, leaving only the banker's lamp on her desk and one square overhead on until she was ready to lock up. From a locked drawer in a rosewood credenza, she swept up the leather tote that held her change of clothes.

Aloha Friday in Honolulu offices meant Casual Friday everywhere, except Keely never deviated from her standard ugly duckling office wear: black horn-rimmed glasses that framed low-prescription lenses, chunky sweaters, bulk-knit skirts, and rubber-heeled shoes.

It helped keep her past where it belonged.

It was after five now and in Keely's book, Aloha Friday meant dinner and cocktails at the Lime Leaf Bistro with two friends she'd known since grade school. She wanted-no, she needed to feel fresh. Pretty. Their after-work get-togethers gave her the time and place to be herself. No guys, or bosses, allowed.

She bolted herself in the main office's private bathroom to change. Jack would leave the office any second now. She could set her watch by him, especially on Fridays. He would sprint out of the office at 5:05 pm on the button, after plotting the sexual downfall of yet another silly female.

Keely removed her sweater, revealing the ultra-soft olivine-green tank-top she wore beneath.

She blew out a breath, cooling off and feeling much more comfortable without the bulky pounds her sweater added to her form. She had gotten flushed and warm in the office listening to Jack's sexy chuckle as he spoke on the phone.

I have connections—yes, of course you do, Mr. Sloane. You *own* J's Beef and Reef, a noisy microbrewery that served steaks flown in from the Big Island!

I'd hoped to take you for a moonlit drive-why of course, Mr. Sloane-only the best for you! Trophy car, trophy girlfriend…

She plucked her glasses from her face, stared at her reflection in the mirror, and wondered how her wide forehead, high cheekbones, and curvy pink mouth would fare pitted up against the women Jack Sloane went for.

"You'd never look twice at me, would you, Mr. Sloane?" she mused out loud. "Too plain, too plump, and half the time I want to kill you."

She cupped her breasts, plumping them up higher than even her sassy red maximizer bra could manage, until her D cups looked ready to spill over the neckline of her tank-top. She liked the way the intense color matched her eyes and, standing in front of the mirror, posed like a pin-up, she almost convinced herself she looked pretty hot-until she heard the office door slam shut and reality bit.

"And off he goes, to spend the night with a girl a bazillion times hotter than I will ever be," she sighed, tucking her glasses into a pocket in her tote. "Have a good night, sir."

She unbuttoned her gray ankle-length wool skirt and slipped it past her hips and off her legs. Legs that were long and shapely, she thought with a sense of pride. At least there was something redeeming about her.

She pulled off her knee-length granny stockings and white support shoes, then tossed the whole nasty lot in a pile before pulling her replacement clothes out of her tote: a tie-dyed cotton miniskirt in ink-bursts of green and royal blue, trimmed with little shiny sequins that matched her tank-top, a blue chambray denim jacket, and beaded slip-on sandals with a short-spiked heel.

She glanced at her watch. *Get a move on, Keely, or you're going to be late!*

She hurried, brushed her teeth, then traced her upper eyelids with nut-brown liner. With a quick, careful hand, she flicked mascara over her lashes and swathed some mango-red gloss over her lips.

She spritzed her neck and stomach with her favorite ginger flower scent, dressed quickly, slid into her sexy sandals, and stuffed her office clothes into the tote.

Oh yes, free at last! She thought, flinging the bathroom door open.

She flipped the bathroom lights off and yanked the pencil out of her bun. Silky waves of autumn-gold hair uncoiled around her shoulders.

"I can be a real woman now—" she declared, but a squeak of surprise escaped her lips when Jack Sloane pushed open the front office door and strode right back in.

Chapter Two

How could he forget his keys?

Jack was glad that his secretary hadn't locked up and left the office yet.

He stopped dead in his tracks.

Standing in his office was a delicious-looking woman who stared straight back at him with a dazzling pair of inky-lashed green eyes that tilted exotically at the corners. Chestnut hair shot with sunlight tumbled in vivid contrast around the blue denim jacket that she wore over a skimpy top.

Jack frowned, noting a vague resemblance to his secretary. Yet…other than sharing similar height and possibly hair color, there was nothing definitive that he could quite pin down. *"Keely?"*

Her mini-skirt hung low on shapely hips and its funky frayed hem rippled against luscious golden thighs. Jack shook his head slowly.

"Definitely *not* my secretary," Jack murmured the comical thought that flashed through his addled brain. This woman might be a cousin, niece, or sister, but *no way* did those legs belong to the quiet office mouse who worked the front desk!

His nostrils flared. The office smelled different, too, like delicate night flowers. *His* secretary didn't wear perfume.

He glanced at the darkened monitor on her desk. Keely was nowhere to be found.

Jack glanced at the lovely stranger and surrendered a hopeless, puzzled smile. "Have we met?"

Her boss's inquiry, coupled with his probing blue stare, gave Keely such a panicked rush that she thought for sure he could hear the blood swooshing around her brain. Oh *no*, she thought, shaking her head at her stupidity. She should have locked the front door.

The dryness shrinking her throat didn't help. She felt like she'd just swallowed the contents of a dust filter.

Time to come clean. The idea made her feel faint. Without the protection of her workday disguise, her own boss didn't recognize her as the dowdy secretary who stayed out of his way whenever he was in the office.

"We haven't met," he asserted, mistaking the shake of her head.

"No, I'm..." she gulped back the tickle in her throat, as Jack waited for her to finish what she was trying to say.

"I'm her..." her throat picked that moment to seize right up, breaking off her confession.

"Cousin?"

She shook her head as she coughed, helpless, unable to correct him. After all, she'd just told him *I'm her*, meaning she was *she*; Keely!

Keely took a tissue from the box he swiped from her desk and extended to her. She dabbed at the corners of her watering eyes.

"Sister?" he queried, trying to be helpful even as he made a split-second decision for her; a choice to tell a little white lie.

Keely grabbed that moment to be the woman that could capture his interest. The way Jack Sloane stared at her made her feel really, really good. The heated masculine interest in his gaze stirred her blood and weakened her legs even as her insides wound up tight.

She nodded.

He smiled.

"So you're Keely's sister, hmm?" He tugged a tissue from the box and moved closer to help her finish patting away the moisture running down her cheek. "All better?" he inquired gently.

Keely nodded and cleared her throat. "Yes. Th-Thanks."

Goosebumps danced down her spine. Her lungs spasmed, suddenly desperate for air. Though Jack was circumspect in the way he dabbed the tissue on her skin, his touch and the subtle, piney scent of him frazzled and excited her down to the tips of her toes.

"I didn't know she had family," he continued. "She doesn't say much. You're both..." his gaze flashed quickly over her, "...very different."

Keely licked her lips and nodded. She didn't dare speak just yet.

He didn't recognize her.

His cunning mind could go a mile a minute, but could not connect the female in front of him with his efficiently dull, undemandingly boring, and quietly blah secretary.

Why was she here? He was bound to ask the question, and her mind worked furiously to manufacture a reason. Better yet, she needed to get out of there pronto.

Damn! Jack glanced at his watch. He still had to go home, shower, change, and pick up Dayna. He'd forgotten about his date once he saw this lovely stranger standing in his office.

He pulled in a breath, wanting to prolong the connection with his secretary's very attractive sister. "Where is she?" he asked, looking around.

"Keely? She's umm…gone."

He frowned.

"She suggested that I apply for a position coming open," she hurriedly explained, "and I showed up late to fill out the application. Keely had to leave, so I promised her I'd lock up when I was through. I hope she won't get into trouble for leaving me here, Mr. Sloane," she added nervously.

"Call me Jack, and no, your sister isn't going to get into any trouble," he assured her. "I'm surprised she had somewhere to go on a Friday night. She often burns the midnight oil."

She tilted her head and tsked. "You don't know much about her, do you?"

Jack shrugged. "She shows up for work every day."

"That's it? That's your requirement for a secretary?" she asked in surprise.

He shook his head. "She came with the place and, truth be told, she's great at her job. She's quiet and undemanding. But," he smiled, "I'd rather discuss more interesting things over dinner. With you," he added with a racy gleam in his sensual blue eyes.

Keely felt her lower body moisten at his words and the unchecked heat that warmed his gaze. He was whip-lash gorgeous, six-feet-three with surfer blond hair streaked by the hot, Hawaiian sun, and bold blue eyes that crinkled at the corners when he grinned. No wonder women went nuts for him.

Even now her pussy juices were oozing onto the thin cotton lining of her little white thong.

Meanwhile, her mind yelled, *bad idea!*

Having dinner with Jack Sloane meant doing other things with him, like squeezing, touching, sucking. Going to bed with him would be the biggest mistake of her life, period.

So what the hell made her say, "I'm available tonight," she had no clue, only that she couldn't take the words back.

"Oh, hell." He closed his amazing eyes for a couple of seconds, sighed, then opened them. "Honey, I've got somewhere I need to be." He grimaced. "A previous engagement. Can I get a rain check?"

This, Keely thought, is getting worse and worse. He was a playboy with a heart!

Jack wasn't going to stand his date up, and that struck a chord inside her. *Get out now*...warned the part of her brain that dealt in common sense...*Before you fall in love with the fool.*

"Sure," she lied. When she left the office, Jack Sloane would never see her like this again. No harm, no foul. She may have to pass on the most exciting sexual experience with a fantasy man, but sacrifices had to be made here.

Keely didn't need any more masquerades. Dealing with him in the office as a certified frump-a-lump was more than enough work for her already.

"Why do I not believe that?" he suddenly asked her.

She darted her tongue out to wet her lips. "I don't know. There will be other opportunities for us to get together, I'm sure." Lies, all lies.

He glanced at her mouth, then at the watch on his wrist, and swore. He wanted to pursue this—pursue her—she could tell, but he had places to go and a woman to see.

If the notorious Jack Sloane magic was at work, he'd have her name, her number, then he'd be off to wine, dine, and sixty-nine his date. Once satisfied, he'd try to work his magic on her.

Keely knew how lethal he could be. She took the phone calls from the angry women. The smart ones soon stopped calling. Others were pathetic and didn't give up.

They sent him flowers, cards, and naked photos through his e-mail. *Too late, you dropped your panties for him on the first date, now he has no more use for you!*

The perfect woman for Jack was someone just like him, someone who wanted him for nothing more than one night of earth-shattering sex before she was on her merry way. Someone he'd never have to see again...

"If I find my keys, will you at least let me give you a ride?" he asked her.

Keely gulped. The temperature in the office shot up ten degrees. Her mind flashed through naughty images of Jack laid out on his back, naked, with his erection poised like a sword while she hovered over him, opening and lowering her body so he sank deep into the grotto of her lush, tight opening.

He looked closely at her. "I meant a ride in my *car*, honey," he said softly, as if sensing her attempt to fantasy-fuck him.

"I-I don't need a ride." she croaked. "Look, don't let me keep you—"

"I've got some time. Just…do me a favor and stay right there. Don't move, please." He started hunting manically around the office for his keys. "I don't want you going anywhere just yet. Did you drive down here?"

His request shot like another arrow into her heart. He even said *please*.

"No, I rode the bus. Here-I'll help you look," she said, desperate to get one of them the heck out of there. Thankfully, she'd dimmed the lights.

She threw her bag in the bathroom and shut the door. Jack prowled through the front office and around her desk, for he often left his sunglasses and keys on her desk while rummaging through his stack of mail.

Keely darted into his office, looking for his keys. There wasn't too much trouble to get into if they stayed in opposite ends of the office.

Nothing on his desk. She looked in the trash can. Nope, not there either. She walked to the guest seating area made up of leather couches and a hickory coffee table hunkered over a pricey wool rug.

Her face burned hot remembering that day three weeks ago. It was a Saturday afternoon and she had gone into the office to research a couple of invoices.

She'd thought it odd that the door to the office was unlocked. She'd been the last one to leave the night before, and she was sure she had locked the door.

Sounds of female cooing came from behind Jack's office door. It wasn't completely closed, so Keely went to investigate. Hotel guests often wandered into the office during daylight hours when they got off on the wrong floor.

Well, it wasn't a couple of lost tourists in Jack's office. A blonde in a red string bikini was leaning back over Jack's desk, her palms spread flat on the desktop.

While she still had her top on, the woman's bikini bottoms were missing and Jack was kneeling in front of her. Her legs were spread and hooked over his broad shoulders.

Keely had clapped a hand to her mouth to smother her shriek of surprise, but couldn't stop staring.

Her boss was lapping at the blonde's pussy with an incredible technique that included a long, skilled tongue flicking at the pink nub of the blonde's clitoris, which was gently pinched between Jack's thumb and forefinger.

Two fingers of his other hand were thrusting between the blonde's thighs in a sexy cock-pump way that nearly made Keely cry out in pleasure herself.

I should leave, she'd thought frantically, but her feet refused to move. Her skin tingled with fierce excitement, and she couldn't help but think: *I love what he's doing and the way he's doing it.*

Keely's nipples hardened into little rosy buds, and her pussy reacted to what she was watching, dripping moisture into her panty.

"I love your mouth, Jack," cried the blonde as she'd wriggled her hips, her large breasts bouncing under the cherry-red triangles as she moved. "Harder...ooh, more!" she'd pleaded, and Jack had obliged, inserting another finger into the blonde's slippery heat and pumping his fingers deep. With the help of his tongue, he drove the blonde just to the brink.

Then he pulled his fingers out.

"No," she cried. "Don't stop!"

Jack still pinched the blonde's clitoris, and she wriggled from all those wild sensations created by his fingers and tongue. Keely understood that need. She had so many unsatisfied needs of her own!

"Not so fast, gorgeous," Jack had murmured in a husky voice. "Tell me what you think of this…" then he clamped his lips over the clit he'd clinched between his fingers and sucked.

The blonde screamed with pleasure, and Keely saw Jack's smile as he paused to nibble the blonde's creaming pussy, lapping against her folds every now and then, but holding back to keep her from climaxing.

"Think you're ready for my cock?" he'd then asked, and the woman nodded, dazed and eager for everything he had to offer. He'd stood, tugged his blue polo shirt up and swept it over his head.

Keely heard the rasp of the zipper on his shorts and decided enough was enough. Time for her to go, even though every lust-filled inch of her ached to stay.

And watch.

She had cast one last longing look at him, then tiptoed backward to her desk to grab her things. She'd scuttled out just as the blonde cried out from Jack's first thrust.

What am I going to do now, Keely agonized, her pussy wet even now, remembering the scene that had kept her awake for many nights.

And, she thought as she leaned over to fluff the jumbo leather pillows on his couch, there was still no sign of the man's damn keys!

He'd also come into the room, rifled through his

desk drawer, and now looked around the loveseat. "I never did get your name," he said, feeling around the edges of the cushions.

"Lei," Keely blurted out her Hawaiian middle name and prayed he'd never seen her personnel file.

"Lovely," he said. He glanced back at her, and she could feel his startled gaze slide from her face and down to her cleavage that was exposed as she leaned over.

"You're not a mainlander, then?" he asked in a strained voice, aiming his gaze back on her face.

Oh dear, Keely thought. He really can be a gentleman when he tries. She quickly straightened. "No. I was born and raised in the islands. Keely and I both," she rushed to add, and turned the other way.

Wrong move. She now felt his gaze warming her ass.

"We're not having too much luck here—"

"I might have to catch a cab—"

They spoke at the same time and turned to each other. Jack looked thoughtful, his gaze studying her. Keely linked her hands in front of her.

"You look disappointed, Mr. Sloane," she said, and smothered back a laugh as she imagined his date's face when he showed up in a dinged-up city cab sporting a fake flower lei on the rearview mirror.

"Damn right," he admitted. "Because I'll have to catch a cab home to Kahala and get my other car."

Keely's smile faded at the mention of his home in a multi-million dollar neighborhood. She had forgotten about his other vehicle—a sleek, brushed nickel Jag. He had the cutest clunker of a truck, too, blue like his eyes, with wood-paneled doors. "My keys will turn up," he continued with an upbeat grin. "But, I hoped to give you a ride wherever you needed to go. Where do you live?"

"Ma—" Keely broke off. She'd been about to say Makiki Heights, a suburb minutes up the road, but that was too close to the truth.

"Makaha," she said, instead, referring to a seaside town on the other side of the island.

"Makaha?" he frowned. "That's all the way out in Timbuc-freaking-tu!"

"I know," she sighed. "So, thanks for the offer, but you see why I can't accept a ride from you—"

"I don't care about that. You caught the bus all the way here from Makaha, and you're taking the bus back? And, you want to work here, in Waikiki? You'll be commuting for hours every day."

"But all the jobs are here in Waikiki," she explained. "At least, for what I do…"

"What position are you applying for?"

"Accountant," she blurted, without thinking. Why didn't she say concierge? She stunk at numbers.

"Hmm. I didn't know we were looking. I'll talk to your sister in the morning. She'll run your background check and, if you meet this hotel's employment criteria, I know of a resort in Makaha that's looking for an accountant. You'll hear from me in the morning. No later than afternoon…"

About a job for my fake sister, Keely thought, feeling her cheeks burn from deceit, even as her heart quaked at the dangerous, exciting game she was playing.

"Just leave your résumé on Keely's desk. I'll fax it over to the manager at The Grove Hotel. If your work ethic is as impressive as your sister's, you should have no problem."

"So, you're happy with Keely's work?" Keely asked him, wondering what else he might say about her.

"Y-e-es," he said, but with a guarded intonation that immediately worried her.

"Um…do you think she could, you know, improve in some areas?" Keely persisted, adding, "I'm new to the hotel industry, you see, and I want to do as good a job as Keely."

His smile was wry. "You'll do fine. Just…do *me* a favor and take her clothes shopping with you. The hotel I'm sending your résumé to has a dress code—resort business casual—and that's all I have to say before I get myself killed."

Keely gulped back the lump in her throat. *Take her clothes shopping with you,* but she heard loud and clear what he wasn't saying.

She—Keely—had set out to look dumpy and succeeded. So why was she feeling hurt that her boss, Mr. Oblivious, actually noticed? Maybe because she was now on the receiving end of his smile, that's why. The way his gaze lingered on her features made her insides simmer and her nipples tighten like spring rose buds…

"Hmm. You're right, Mr. Sloane. I just don't think Keely's got a lot of money to spend on clothes and make-up—"

Jack threw his head back and laughed. "My ass! I doubled her wages, along with everyone else's, when I came on board."

Keely blushed, thinking of his ass and the perfect shape it presented in tailored trousers. "Did you *really*?

Of course you know that Hawaii is one of the most expensive places in the United States to live. I'm sure if you gave her a raise and called it something like 'clothing allowance' you would see an improvement in my-my *sister's* appearance."

He was still smiling as he studied her face, and Keely sucked in a breath as the wetness between her legs trickled through the crotch of her panties.

"You've given me something to think about, Lei."

"You do that," Keely said. "Well, I'm sorry I wasn't much help with your keys. I should go."

He nodded and stepped aside for her to pass. When she did, the spiky little heel of her sandals caught on something on the wool rug and sent her tripping, right into Jack Sloane's arms.

Chapter Three

This night, Jack thought as Lei toppled into him, is getting better and better. Caught off guard himself, he fell backward into the couch and took her down with him.

Neither moved. Jack lay against the cushions and as he held a stunned Lei in his arms, he savored the smell of her hair and thought of misty island rains. Then he wondered how fast he could capitalize on the luscious curves making themselves at home against the hard nooks and crannies of his body.

She stared down into his face, as startled as he. Sensation rippled beneath his skin from the physical warmth, pleasurable sight, and exotic smell of her.

Jack couldn't stand it anymore. He slid his hands up from her waist and trawled his fingers through her hair, bringing her head down to meet his mouth. His lips found hers, soft and pillowy, and fireworks began to sizzle.

He'd have stopped if she got mad and smacked him.

Instead, she kissed him right back with a wild-hot passion. She kissed him like a starving little sex fiend hungry for his mouth, and so much more, by the way she moved her hips and rubbed against his erection. The friction of their clothes heightened the excitement and the hope, at least on Jack's part, that they would be able to take them off at some point.

"I tripped on your keys," she groaned against his mouth, rubbing her breasts over his chest. "They're on the floor, so you'd better get them and go."

"I'd better," he murmured, grabbing the opening of her jacket and peeling it away from her shoulders. Impatiently she shrugged the jacket off, refusing to break the connection of their kiss.

In turn, she tugged at the lapels of his sport coat, which he removed without having to break their heated lip-lock. He flung his coat out of the way and reached out to squeeze her breasts, his fingers flicking over the outline of her distended nipples, nipples he wanted so badly to suck.

He slipped down the strap of her top and her bra, reached in and cupped a breast, shocked by how plump, lush and warm it felt inside his palm. She moaned. Her breath fluttered against his skin, teasing at the need in his body.

Neither seemed headed out the door anytime soon.

Suddenly, his cell phone buzzed inside his jacket.

"Hell," Jack said.

Lei went still in his arms, too. Much as he would have loved to ignore the call, he fished his phone out of his jacket just as Lei picked his keys up off the floor and dropped them in his lap, grinning at the massive lump created by his erection.

He breathed a sigh of relief when she left the room. His date was on the line, and she was waiting. Jack promised he'd be there, hung up, and went looking for the beautiful stranger. He wanted her number, and no way was he letting her leave until he had it.

She was gone. No trace of her in the lounge, the little copy room, the reception area inside the office. She wasn't out in the hall, and the sitting area where the bank of elevators opened up to was empty.

Jack searched Keely's desk for a copy of Lei's job application. Nothing.

He hadn't dreamt her. Her perfume lingered on his skin, his clothes. He wasn't imagining his raging-hard cock or the desire that buzzed throughout his body.

Jack sighed and made his decision. Dinner with Dayna, then he'd drop her off at home. The woman he desperately wanted to make love to had disappeared into thin air.

His secretary would know how to get hold of her. He had no doubt about that.

8:01 a.m. Monday morning

"I'm sorry, Mr. Sloane, I don't know how to get hold of her," Keely broke the news to him. She'd stepped into the office earlier to a ringing phone with Jack on the other end of the line, anxious to get moving on her *sister's* background check.

No doubt he'd gotten lucky on Friday night, while she had been a mental wreck after running out of the office. She'd taken the stairwell to avoid waiting for an elevator. On her way to the Lime Leaf, she'd skulked around hibiscus hedges, palm trees. She'd blended in with crowds-anything for cover just in case Jack was sitting in traffic nearby.

"Keely, she's your sister."

"Er, sure. But...she's always losing her cell phone and I'm forced to leave messages at any number of places where she might be staying."

Silence.

Keely smiled. *What do you think of your prospective job applicant now, Mr. Sloane?* Keely wondered, hoping he'd immediately lose interest.

His deep laugh vibrating across the phone took her by surprise. "So she's a little bohemian," he mused. "Look, I'm on my way in, but run that background check as soon as possible. Please."

"So, you'd hire her? Just like that?"

"We-e-ll, no. *I* wouldn't. A friend of mine runs a resort out in Makaha and has agreed to take her on if she wants to work someplace closer to home, doing the same job she came here to apply for. And since when did we need an accountant?" he asked. "We use Kalani-Keeler."

"I-she might have misunderstood. We're looking for a front desk hospitality rep."

"That's what I thought. Well, it doesn't matter. We'll find a good fit for her somewhere…"

Just not at this hotel, Keely thought, and knew exactly why Jack was pushing Lei in the other direction. It wasn't for altruistic reasons. Jack kept his lovers—or potential lovers—outside the workplace, thank goodness.

She'd worked in offices where the boss slept with everything in a skirt, and hated the secretive looks and sexy banter that went on.

She also knew firsthand the heartache of being accused of sleeping with the boss. She shuddered at memories that seemed to forever taunt her, and looked down at the clothes she wore; thrift store specials and the ugliest fat-heeled arch-support shoes that money could buy.

If Jack's girlfriends ever saw her, they'd never

have to worry about him making moves on his secretary.

"I'll see what I can do, Mr. Sloane," Keely said, and hung up.

8:27 a.m.

"Any luck?" Jack asked as he browsed the mail on Keely's desk. He'd come into the office ten minutes ago, settled himself at his desk with a cup of coffee and, when he couldn't psyche himself out to work, he roamed over to her desk to check the mail.

He couldn't stop thinking about Keely's sister, Lei. She'd occupied his mind so much that he'd passed on a night of uninhibited sex with Dayna who—once she took a look at his roadster—was all over him like a rash.

He should have backed out of the date and stayed with Keely's sister, but he had a bit of class. He knew what it was like to be stood up. His ex-fiancée had given him the lesson from hell, leaving Jack a commitment-phobe ever since. But, if nothing else, he always kept promises.

At least one good thing came out of that date with Dayna. It made him realize that he did desire a relationship—with Lei.

Since he'd dropped Dayna off at the curb of her high-rise apartment, Dayna had left seven messages on his cell. Funny, he hadn't been worthy of her time when he had on jeans and an old T-shirt. He wondered if Lei was the cool, calculating type.

No way to know but to find out for himself, he decided, unable to stay focused in his office. His gaze kept straying to the couch where he'd kissed her, where she'd kissed him back, where she'd rubbed him up and down with her amazing breasts. Oh, the plans he had for those breasts…

"I sent her an e-mail, Mr. Sloane. Not sure how current her e-mail address is, though," mumbled his secretary, now bent over the copier. She was always so busy doing something that she never quite seemed to talk to him face to face, or look him in the eye.

"She said you told her about the job," he pressed on.

"I hope you don't mind. It's just that I hear from her every now and then, when she's between jobs. She…ah, she doesn't stay at jobs very long."

"I can see why. Some jerk probably hits on her every ten minutes," Jack replied, undeterred.

There was no response to that, he noted, and watched as she moved from the copier to the fax machine with her head down and her back to him. She had an interesting walk, Jack thought, graceful and unrushed. He wondered how old she really was.

He cleared his throat and studied a marketing brochure. "I was thinking…are you due for a raise anytime soon?"

"No, sir. You gave me a raise when you took over the hotel."

"Hm, well, I've decided to issue checks for an annual clothing allowance for administrative staff. I'll give you a list of names. Cut a check for…" he named a figure that he considered more than fair. He heard her gasp. "What? Should it be more?"

"Umm…if you threw in another five hundred dollars, that would be fine," she said in a hoarse little voice.

"Okay," he said. "I'll be in my office for the rest of

the morning."

8:49 a.m.

Jack Sloane, Keely fumed as he buzzed her extension, was going to drive her up the flipping wall!

She ignored him, knowing there would be no rest for him now, or anyone else for that matter. Once he was in pursuit of a woman, nothing stood in his way.

She tried to dissuade him by hinting that Lei was a free-spirit, a job-hopper, but he didn't care. When Jack Sloane wanted a woman, he got her.

Since *Lei* had worked him into such good spirits, Keely had recklessly tacked that ridiculous five hundred dollars on to his already ridiculously high clothing allowance just to test his mood. Yet Jack didn't even blink over the higher dollar figure.

She finally picked up the line as she had done four times since he'd locked himself in his office twenty minutes ago and said, "She's not e-mailed me back, yet, sir."

"I see," he said.

"But not to worry. You'll be the first person I tell if she does," she told him with mild sarcasm.

"Yes, thank you," he replied drily. "I just e-mailed you that list, by the way."

"Yes, sir," Keely said. She clicked on his e-mail and opened it up.

There was only one name on the list.

Hers.

She sent the phone crashing down on Jack Sloane's rotten ears.

That'll fix you, you little vixen, Jack thought as he hung up the phone. *Wanna shake out another five hundred bucks from me for a clothing allowance? Fine.*

You'd just better not be looking like a bag lady anymore!

He drummed his fingers on his desk. Desperation, he knew, was really setting in if messing with his secretary was giving him his biggest thrill of the morning. He grinned. She was kind of fun to tease, he thought, just as his personal line rang.

"Sloane," he greeted. The last thing he expected to hear was Lei's sexy voice on the other line, and the sound made every pulse point in his body leap like crazy.

"Hi, Jack. Keely said you were trying to reach me…?"

"Yes I was," he said, and smiled. "I am going to kiss my secretary for tracking you down." The vision of his secretary squinting up at him behind those ugly-ass glasses made him think twice. "Maybe not."

"Be nice," Lei warned with a light laugh. "She's still my sister."

"Fine. I'll be nice. How are you, Lei? Did you make it home safe and sound?"

"Yes, thank you."

"I've got some good news. The job at The Grove Hotel in Makaha is still available."

"Oh, my-you're a mover and a shaker, Mr. Sloane," she murmured, and Jack closed his eyes as her soft voice unwound him like a steam bath.

"Honey, you'd be shocked," he murmured right back. "So if you bring your application over, I'll fax it to my contact."

"Is it possible for me to fax my application over to you instead?" she asked. "It's just that I'm in Makaha, and it'll take at least two hours for me to get to your office."

Jack snapped the pencil he was using to doodle on his calendar in two. He wanted to see this woman so badly he could taste it.

"You could do that, I suppose, but I was looking forward to seeing you, taking you to lunch, maybe. Or dinner." He'd drive over to Makaha to get her. He just needed her. Jack pulled in a deep breath. Her silence wasn't helping. "I just can't seem to get you out of my head."

"Really?"

His ears, his mind, and other body parts perked at the wistful sound in her voice. "Really. I loved being with you, touching you. And those sounds you made each time we kissed kept me from a good night's sleep—" he broke off, damn near confessing how he'd masturbated every time he imagined her touch, how turned on he'd been thinking about her, anticipating the moment that they would meet again. He had counted the ways he was going to touch, lick, and stroke her skin, her body, if given a chance.

He'd imagined the things he would do to her pussy with his teeth, mouth, and tongue, after he nibbled on her earlobe and whispered his erotic plans. The only thing his cock had slammed into since meeting her was his damned hand.

"Look, if you tell me to buzz off, I'll still forward your résumé to my contact. Even Keely will tell you that I don't like to waste anyone's time. I'll have her e-mail you the job description and you can go from there. Sound good?"

"Mr. Sloane, I-I really appreciate all you're doing, all you've done…it's just that I-"

Son of a bitch! Jack didn't want to hear the "but" that was coming, so he spared them both further awkwardness by saying simply, "Take care, Lei," and hanging up.

He glanced at his watch and wondered how long it was going to take to get his cock to stand down. Thwarted lust, he thought, totally sucked.

He picked up the phone and buzzed his secretary. It took her a while to pick up and when she did, for a split second she sounded soft, almost like Lei. Of course he knew better. It was just his mind longing for something he couldn't have. "Something's wrong, Keely."

Chapter Four

Keely held the phone to her ear with a shaking hand. She'd just dashed in after standing outside of the office, masquerading on her cellular as Lei. Lei, who so badly wanted what Jack was offering—no holds barred lust and sexy loving. She certainly wasn't getting it from anyone else.

The things he said—admitting how he lost sleep—played on her heartstrings. She couldn't even give him a decent brush off. She'd tried to, but he wouldn't let her. As usual, Jack was in control and she wanted to stomp on his stupid list.

He was so tender with her sister, *Lei*, and such a damned rat to his secretary, *Keely*. He knew she had pushed the clothing allowance thing the whole time! She had no other choice but to admit the truth. Jack Sloane was clever, lovable, gorgeous, sexy, sneaky...

"What are you talking about, Mr. Sloane?" she asked, breathless.

"Your sister just called. I'm trying to ask her out, you know, on a date. I'd even settle for lunch, but she doesn't seem interested."

Keely swallowed. After the way Lei behaved the other night on his couch, no wonder he was confused.

"What's her story? Is she married? Got a boyfriend?"

"No, Mr. Sloane. I think she had a past experience with a guy that didn't want to commit. He was something of a player." *Like you.*

"After you left on Friday, she was here and we…connected. I know I wasn't imagining things…"

Perspiration beaded on Keely's forehead at the memory of her breasts filling his palms, the satiny feel of her nipples as they rasped against his skin, his tongue teasing and exploring her mouth, his teeth biting down gently on her lower lip.

How she had dreamed these past three nights of what they *didn't* do on his couch, and what it would have been like to go down on him, to pull his cock out of his trousers. He was a big, bad bruiser, too. She could tell by the way his erection had filled the space between her thighs when she'd rubbed her pussy against his shaft.

Her body juices from that night were probably still clinging to his trousers. She closed her eyes. "Connected? L-Like what do you mean, Mr. Sloane?"

"There was chemistry there. Man-woman, you know? Forget it. You wouldn't understand—"

"Try me."

"Should I even be saying anything to you? You're her sister—"

"I might be able to help," she coaxed, desperate to hear what he had to say, desperate to know how she-*Lei*-made him feel.

"Truth be told, I took one look at her and my heart went ka-pow."

"And then what happened?" Keely asked, lifting her skirt.

"We wound up on my couch, that's what

34

happened."

Keely opened her thighs just wide enough to slide her finger into the silky wetness that already soaked her panties. Knowing he was on the other end of the line, hearing his voice, was making her nipples swell and her clitoris throb.

"What? You sat down with her on the couch?" she asked, her forefinger rubbing past the inner lips that ruffled around her clitoris, her mind spinning with sexy tension.

"She tripped and fell, and we tumbled onto my couch."

"Did you like that?"

There was a pause. "Well, sure."

Keely bit her lip, squirmed in her plush leather chair just so, giving her fingers access to her wetness.

"But the question is did Lei like it?" he countered.

"Mm-hmm." Keely murmured, imagining it was his tongue buried inside of her because Jack's cock would be huge. "I mean—I'm sure she did."

"Yeah. She did. At least, I thought so at the time."

Keely gulped as excitement coiled and uncoiled deep inside her body, sensation twisting higher and higher. She flicked her clit with her thumb, back and forth, gently, softly, imagining it was Jack's tongue there, swirling around, tasting her... "What made you think that, sir?"

"Well, she started to pull my clothes off..."

Keely hit the mute button and exhaled a little moan, her finger working steadily, quickly now. Her hips gyrated, and she quietly drowned in the pleasurable danger of Jack's voice, her fingers, and an unlocked door. He could walk out any minute. She undid the mute feature.

"Did you stop her?" Her voice shook a little as her fingers moved faster and faster, her heart racing as her body prepared itself for the strike of bliss about to hit.

"No, and she didn't stop me either when I kissed her, and…" he trailed off, but the silence of his thoughts was enough to send her over the edge.

Knowing he was thinking about Lei, about them together that night on his office couch was enough to send Keely crashing. She bit her lip as her finger circled over and around her clitoris, and she came, and came, and came, her mind whispering his name.

"…and," Jack said abruptly, "gentlemen don't kiss and tell. Have I told you enough to assure you that I would like to get to know your sister?"

Her mind floated back down. "Mm-hmm," she said, ripples of her climax ebbing gently from her body. She patted her skirt into place.

"So, what are we going to do about it?"

"We? Who's we?" Keely asked, confused.

"We two. Me and you. You and me. What do I do? Send her flowers? Exotic sweets? Would Lei like that?"

Keely rested her cheek in her palm and smiled. "Oh, she would like that a lot, Mr. Sloane!"

"Roses. The flowers have to be roses."

"Hmm. A nice mix of dusky pinks, plum, all colors of blue, and cream, I think. Oh, and white-chocolate dipped Sunset Tango cherries from La Petite Sweets. They're her favorite."

Jack chuckled. "I see this is going to cost me a pretty penny, but your sister is worth it. Where do I send them?"

Keely froze. She hadn't given a thought to an

address. She could just kick herself! She might be forced to produce Lei sooner than she wanted. "Oh, I was thinking…it would be a good idea to just send it here, and I'll deliver them to her myself."

"Why can't I just send the roses and cherries directly to her?"

"Because, Mr. Sloane, I know you want it. Her address, I mean. Let me talk her into coming down and dropping off her application. Having the flowers and fruit here will be an extra surprise when she arrives, and will warm her right up about the idea of having lunch or dinner with you. Er, what if she still doesn't want to go out with you?"

"What?" he asked, shell-shocked at the thought.

"What if you don't get a return on your investment?"

"Let me worry about that. You worry about getting Lei in here. Please."

She smiled. "I'll do that, Mr. Sloane." Keely hung up, and minutes later Jack buzzed her again.

"Because of the colors, the roses won't be delivered until the day after tomorrow. Late afternoon."

Good, Keely thought. She'd picked the rarest color roses to find on the island and was banking on more time; time to figure Lei out of the mess Keely had gotten her-*them*-into.

"Let me e-mail Lei again and ask her if she can come in Wednesday afternoon."

He said nothing.

"Mr. Sloane, are you okay?"

"I can't see this woman until Wednesday. What do you think?"

You've got two days worth of cold showers, that's

what I think! Keely wanted to say, but she couldn't even find humor in that. She'd be taking cold showers, too!

She didn't know who was being punished more, Jack or herself. The laugh was on her, now.

Jack wanted the mysterious Lei, and the quickest way to lose his interest, Keely thought wickedly, was for Lei go to bed with him.

Chapter Five

5:45 p.m. Wednesday

The ladies room outside the office, Keely decided, was the perfect place for a quick-change artist. It was low-lit, quiet, and stocked with everything from lotion to fluffy hand towels.

This was the executive floor and everyone else-save for the night crew downstairs at the concierge desk-were gone.

Jack's flowers had been delivered earlier. In a separate, clear-lidded box, four juicy-fat golden-pink cherries with long stems nestled in their white chocolate cloaks. The cherries were an ultra sweet, extra-large Northwest variety that she'd always wanted to try, but at twenty-four dollars a pound she could only afford to press her nose against the chocolatier's window and drool.

"Lei will be here after five," Keely had told Jack that morning. "I'll leave the door unlocked, just in case I'm gone. You'll still be here, won't you?"

He'd nodded. "Sure."

Well, duh. Of course.

Getting Lei alone with Jack was the point, but he had not said much the past two days. It was almost like he'd pushed Lei to the back of his mind.

Keely nibbled on her lower lip, nervous. She

hadn't seen Jack since he left for lunch after noon. He had yet to come back.

She tugged the hem of her white denim halter mini-dress further down her thighs, picked up her tote bag that held her office clothes, and stuffed it under the vanity where it wouldn't be noticed. She plucked a gardenia from one of the fresh arrangements, stuck the bloom behind her right ear, and walked down the hall to the Island Lily's office suites.

She stepped inside and knew right away he wasn't there. She could always catch the piney edge of his cologne whenever he was in.

Oh no. He really had gotten bored. He wasn't planning on coming back.

The lights were still turned low, as she deliberately left them earlier. The roses were on her desk, the cherries in their gold foil box with its clear lid and sheer pink ribbon undisturbed.

It was just as well. Nothing would have come of a sexual interlude with Jack, except fabulous sex.

She buried her nose in the jewel-colored roses, then pulled a creamy blossom from the bunch to take home with her.

This was the end of the road for Lei. Jack was never meant to meet her anyway, Keely thought. Resigned, she opened the door to leave only to find Jack standing on the other side.

His shades were on his handsome face, and his hands were full with take-out bags from J's. He'd changed into black cargo pants and wore an offbeat yellow-green-black plaid shirt with a black T-shirt underneath. He smelled so good and looked hella sexy!

"Leaving so soon?" he drawled.

This time her heart went ka-pow at the smile that curved his lips. She could feel his gaze eating her up, from her face to her pink toenails, and back up to her face with a slight pause where her breasts bumped together behind her halter-top.

Oh, and you can just forget about any exit strategies tonight, Lei!

"There was n-nobody here," she stammered. "I-I thought everyone had left for the night."

"And you were going to leave without your goodies?"

"These were for me?" she asked, and blushed at her shameless acting.

He looked at the creamy rose she twirled in her hand. "Yes."

She brought the flower up to her nose. "Well, good. Now I don't feel so bad that I planned to take this one with me."

He smiled. "Interesting. Of all the colors there, you went for the plainest one," he observed, thinking, no doubt, how he'd paid out the ying-yang for the rarest roses that she'd simply ignored in favor of the plainest, sweetest smelling one.

She nodded, happy. "It's my favorite."

"So are white chocolate covered cherries, I'm told. What do you like to eat?"

"Whatever's in that bag? It smells good," she said, her stomach growling. She hadn't been able to eat at all today for thinking of the night to come.

"I was hoping you'd say that."

She took one of the bags from him and pushed the door back so he could pass. This was a side of her boss she'd never seen: the brash, casual, after-hours side

41

when the brash office executive was all she'd ever known.

And…she thought, mouth watering, she hoped to see a lot more of him tonight.

Jack spread a tablecloth over the coffee table in his office. From the same bag the tablecloth came from, he drew out two glass candleholders and lit the tea lights that came with them.

"I guess this means I'm staying for dinner?" Lei asked, and gave him the bag she held. She was everything and more than he'd dreamt about these past few nights.

He gave her a wicked smile. Something in his eyes must have warned her that she might be the main course because she stared straight back at him, bit her lip, and then lowered her lashes.

"I'll go get the flowers," she mumbled. She didn't, thank God, run out the door.

I'm falling in love with this girl, he thought, and frowned as he set out the wineglasses, remembering what happened the last time he gave his heart to a woman.

His mouth tightened. Jack didn't know anything about Lei, but he intended to fix all that tonight. He also intended to stay in control.

She brought in the roses and the cherries. As she set the flowers on one end of the low-lying table, Jack grabbed a couple of couch pillows and tossed them on the rug. He waited while she removed the lid from the cherries, releasing the fragrance of the chocolate and fruit.

Jack took her hand in his and sat her down on a cushion in front of the feast laid out before them:

luscious morsels of assorted sushi and sashimi on little red lacquer platters lined with glossy ti leaves, pickled young ginger, and lemon slices.

She toed her heels off and made herself comfortable on the pillow while he poured chilled plum wine into glasses. He took his place on the cushion across from her, handed her a wine glass, then picked up the only set of chopsticks.

"Pick out what you'd like first, Lei."

She couldn't take her eyes off him.

"The food, honey."

She blinked, "Oh, yes. The food...umm..." she pointed to the grilled unagi.

"Eel—one of my favorites," he said, picking it up with the chopsticks. She leaned forward and opened her mouth.

The image of something else sliding past her lips flashed through Jack's mind as she bit into the sushi. He ate the other half, and wondered how he was going to get through this meal without losing his mind.

He took a sip of his wine. She surprised him by taking the chopsticks. "Your turn," she said.

He studied the platter, and then pointed to a diamond shaped slice filled with rice, avocado, crab, paper thin slices of English cucumber, and dotted with a peppery sauce that was sprinkled with orange fish roe. Using the chopsticks, she tapped a dab of wasabi onto the sushi, picked it up with skillful ease, and fed him the entire piece.

She did the same for herself, but again bit the sushi in half, savored the tastes, then ate the other half.

"Mmm, spicy," she said, and took a long, lazy sip of her wine.

He watched her throat as she swallowed. Jack's cock hardened with his yearning to touch her. Kiss her. Possess her.

"Do you like spice?" Jack asked, swirling his wine in his glass.

She nodded. Her gaze met his and she asked, "Do you think feeding each other might be easier if I brought my pillow over next to you?"

He shrugged. They were hardly experiencing any difficulties, but he liked the idea of having her next to him. "We could try it and see."

She pushed her pillow under the table to the other side next to him. Jack yanked it even closer, and when he did, a strong, erotic musk rose to greet him. His nostrils flared at the intoxicating musk of her pussy. She wanted him—was *wet* for him. His mouth watered and he struggled to compose his thoughts.

Hard to do, he thought, watching as she crawled toward him on her hands and knees, looking like a sleek, exotic animal. Her gaze locked on his, acknowledging both his power and her submission.

She was his if he wanted her. He reached out and pulled her closer.

"To hell with the pillow," he growled in her ear, a sweet white flower adorning it. "I want you on my lap—" and then he kissed her mouth, spiced with the salty tang of roe.

Mingled with the wine, it was like nectar of the gods, and he dipped his tongue into her mouth for more. The capsaicin from the pepper added a warmth that spread across both their palates.

She trembled and squirmed, her butt settling comfortably on his lap, and she brought her fingers up to the buttons of his shirt, working quickly to tug them from their holes. He helped her remove his shirt and yanked the black T-shirt he wore underneath from the waistband of his pants, tossing that aside as well.

She smiled and licked her lips as she touched his arms and muscled chest. She leaned over and kissed his shoulder, all the while stroking the back of his neck with her fingers.

Jack snaked a hand up behind her neck to pop the snaps of her halter while his arm closed around her waist. He buried his face in her neck and breathed in her scent. It was no secret his cock was hard.

Luckily, he held a woman who felt its probing demand against her butt cheeks and, judging by the shallow breaths that marked the rise and fall of her breasts, liked it.

She blew softly into his ear, which sent more blood rushing from his head down to his penis.

"What else do you want to eat?" she whispered, and bit his ear lobe.

"I can't wait another second," Jack muttered, and tossed her with gentle force down on the pillow. "You'd better not be teasing, sweetheart," he warned. The straps holding her halter- top up over her breasts fell away and exposed her breasts.

She yanked the straps down to her waist and brought her hands up to cup her breasts, offering them to him. "Teasing...you mean, like this?"

He groaned. "Your nipples, they're like little cherries." He bent his head and took one in his mouth, loving the sound of the pleasured sigh that escaped her lips.

His hands covered hers. Together they squeezed

her breasts, his hands maneuvering over hers to give those mounds of pink-tipped flesh a tantalizing jounce before bending his head to lick and suck on each one.

Jack couldn't get enough of her, sucking each nipple, aureole, and as much of her flesh deep into his mouth. One of his hands left hers to pull her skirt up above her golden thighs, sliding up to squeeze a naked buttock.

"Your skin's like silk," he murmured, and wondered if she was totally naked underneath.

He got his answer when he felt the strap of a thong in the cleft of her ass cheeks. He looked forward to brushing aside the crotch of her thong so he could dip his tongue into her…

"Jack, please kiss me," she pleaded.

He gazed into her eyes. "You're asking for it, you know that?"

She smiled up at him and crossed her hands behind her head. "Begging."

Jack shook his head. "Begging involves you being on your knees."

"I can do that, too."

He groaned, kissed her mouth, and moved down her body.

Chapter Six

I'm going to come, and he hasn't even taken my clothes off, Keely thought helplessly, squirming as he kissed his way down her skin. His fingers flicked over and around her nipples, which were still wet from his mouth. He shoved the hem of her skirt up to her waist to reveal her flat stomach and the dainty belly button pink pearl piercing.

He saw it and she could feel his mouth curve into a smile against her skin.

"Do you like my pearl?" she whispered.

"Mm-hmm. Both of them."

"Both of them?"

"This one…" he kissed her belly button, "…and this one," he shoved aside the crotch of her thong, slid his tongue down the cleft of her pussy, and found her clitoris.

Her moan of shock and delight filled the room as his fingers moved slickly around her pussy lips, over and around his working tongue to heighten her excitement. She could hardly breathe and panted just to keep from crying out when he bored his tongue deep inside her wet pleasure sheath.

He spread her thighs even wider, tongue thrusting deep and then pulling out to flick his tongue across her clit.

His moves were so bold and stunning, she knew she couldn't take much more without crashing. "Stop, Jack, please," she pleaded, even as her body burned for him to take her all the way.

He rose and lay alongside her. "Don't you want to come?" he asked gently, watching as she caught her breath.

She nodded. "With you," and thought she'd die when he caressed her cheek with his forefinger. She could smell her musk on his fingers and wanted, no, needed to smell and taste him, too.

"We have all night, Lei."

"Then I'd better take matters into my own hands," she said, and prodded a pillow under his head. She reversed their roles and, with a smug grin, took control.

She stood up and let her dress fall at her feet, blushing when he let out a wolf whistle. She kicked the dress off to the side and nearly tripped in her nervousness.

"Easy…"

"Sorry! I don't make it a habit of stripping in front of men."

"I can tell. I like it." He clasped his hands behind his head. A thoughtful gleam brightened his blue eyes.

Keely gazed down at him, sprawled on the carpet, his hard shaft parachuting his pants. He looked like a feast, with his golden-tanned skin and bulging chest muscles.

She dropped to her knees and leaned over to kiss him, her hair falling around them like a satin cloak. He made kissing feel like hot, sensual *fucking*, only with their mouths, lips, and tongues—rubbing, touching and teasing. When he squeezed her naked breasts, his fingers pinching at her nipples, sexy little bolts of lightning charged right to her pulsing clit.

Her fingers undid the button on his pants. She pulled down his zipper and sighed as her fingers made contact and closed over the large roll of his silky-skinned cock.

"It feels so…big. I want to see it!" she pleaded against Jack's mouth. She freed him from his pants.

She ran lazy fingers over the length of his penis, admiring him shamelessly—all that golden skin and the engorged head of his perfect cock. If one night was all she'd ever have of Jack Sloane, she would take all she could get.

Jack struggled for air as Lei kissed him deeply and caressed his stone-stiff cock with her fingers, scraping the sensitive area an inch beneath his balls with her fingernails. The sensual strokes made him groan.

Then something ultra soft took the place of her fingers. She rubbed the rose along his cock, around his testicles, and down just beneath his sacs where she'd lightly scraped with her fingernails earlier.

His deep, pleasured "mmm" filled the room, and Lei's lips moved down his body as her fingers manipulated that plump, fragrant rose around his balls, his thighs.

When her mouth closed over the tip of his cock, a powerful growl rumbled from his chest.

The hand he stroked her hair with twined and clenched into the strands as she suckled and licked his shaft, her head moving up and down as she took his length deep into her mouth until he could feel the tight tension of her throat, tongue, and cheeks working to pleasure him.

"You are so-o-o good, baby," he murmured, and gritted his teeth, mentally pushing back the urge to pull her up, spread her open, and plunge his tongue into her pussy.

She continued to suckle him with her mouth. She squeezed and jiggled his balls, then licked them. "Mmm...just like that..." Jack said softly, just before her lips crowned his cock, glistening with his pre-cum and the saliva from her mouth.

"Enough," he said, and drew her up to him.

"Don't you want to...?"

"Hell yes, but I thought we'd have a sample of dessert," he said, and turned her on her back, leaning over to retrieve a cherry.

Jack enjoyed the way her eyes went wide and her lips curled into a saucy little smile. Still clutching the rose, she twirled it beneath her nose, her gaze teasing.

"Whatcha doing with that?" she asked, and watched as he bit into it.

"Just melting the chocolate," he said, and placed the cherry on her tummy, below her belly button pearl, juicy side down.

He cupped her breast in his large hand, squeezing the orb and rubbing her nipple against his lips, kissing and suckling. With his other hand, he moved the half-eaten cherry down between her thighs, then cupped it over her little sex bud, pressing the fruit over her pink flesh, flavoring her by moving the fruit softly over the engorged tip.

She panted, breathless—Jack knew—with sensation.

His cock ached to be buried deep inside her pussy, creaming and ready for him, and for his tongue to fill her mouth. With his thumb, he lightly massaged her clitoris before thrusting his forefinger into her lush, wet opening.

"I want you, Jack. Now!"

He shook his head, his eyes staring into hers. "Not yet."

He kissed her, then replaced his mouth with the cherry, oozing warm white chocolate across her lips. She licked and tasted her musky pussy juices as they mingled with the sweet, fragrant cherry and chocolate.

She buried her fingers in his hair as he slid down her body. His fingers swept her scrap of a thong off her hips and down her legs. He separated her plump labia lips with anxious fingers, his eyes admiring her silky hairless mound as he flicked her pussy's inner folds that cloaked her hidden pearl. With his tongue, he licked and lapped at it.

"Mmm. I love the way you taste, baby," he murmured, and the vibration of his mouth and his fevered breath on her skin made her purr.

Jack was relentless, shaping his tongue under her clitoris and hooding it with his upper lip. He sucked softly. Keely's hips surged. She half-moaned, half-sobbed his name as he eased his fingers inside the slick, tight walls of her vagina.

"Jack," she pleaded, squeezing his broad shoulders. "I want your cock. Come into me now. Please!"

He would not stop. She was about to crumble, but just as he felt her tense, hurtling toward an orgasm, he stopped and slipped a condom over his penis. He poised over her, rubbed the tip of his cock around her vagina for moisture, then thrust deep into her pleasure box.

Her eyes flew wide at the way he filled her. "Oh

my God, Jack. You're huge."

He stared down at her. "And you're really tight. Am I hurting you?"

"Just my feelings if you don't start giving it to me," she murmured, moving her hips in slow, sweet gyrations.

Jack moved in a rhythm that was slow and deep. "You feel this, baby?"

She nodded, hardly able to speak.

"I'm getting you acquainted with my cock, inch by inch. The way it feels, the way it fits inside you, how deep it can go—oh, yeah. You can take almost all of me, sweetheart."

"Yes," she gasped.

Jack closed his eyes, feeling her uterus crown the turgid tip of his cock.

He reached down and diddled her clit with his forefinger, not missing a stroke. Keely cupped her breasts, flicking and pinching her nipples beneath his gaze, both held in the grip of seduction and lust.

Slowly Jack fucked her, his groans and her sighs filling the cozy confines of the room, and then he planted his hands on either side of her shoulders, bracing himself.

He picked up the beat of his hips, increasing speed and tempo so that his cock pistoned in and out of her cunt. They both looked down where they joined, enjoying the erotic images of Jack's cock disappearing in and out of her pussy.

The rose dropped from Keely's hand when she reached down and grabbed his balls, stroking the narrow muscle under them before gripping and squeezing his sacs. His growl filled her ears, goading her to touch herself, too.

She rubbed her clitoris, as her breasts bounced with each thrust of his cock and, when she knew she was going to come, she stopped rubbing.

She wrapped her legs around Jack's waist and ran her fingers across the plane of his cheekbones, flagged red with lust and desire. He turned his head to suck the finger that had pleasured her clitoris, and the swirl of his tongue lapping at the moisture nearly made her faint.

And...oh God! There it was, that sweet, magical *spark*.

His cock coaxed it from the powerhouse of her clitoris. Jack's pistoning moves took control of her pleasure, pushing her—and himself—from spark to flame.

"Oooh...Jack, oh yesss!" she cried in surging bliss. "I love the way you move..."

He grunted, a harsh yet sexy sound, and sped up the beat of his hips. The sucking wet sounds of his sex sinking and pounding into her sheath mimicked their moans and groans of pleasure.

"Lei...come, sweetheart," he murmured, and crushed his mouth to hers as she hit the breaking point.

He shocked her by pulling out and quickly twirling his tongue around her pulsating clit, then thrust deep into her silky wet cunt again and again as pure sensation seized her up and then quaked through her mind and body.

Sensation exploded as his cock rubbed exquisitely against her clit. Pleasure pounded into her from all sides, inside and out. There was no escape.

Chapter Seven

Jack couldn't think of anything but the mind-blowing feel of being inside Lei, her lovely face inches beneath his, and her eyes closed in ecstasy. Moisture filmed her skin and her cheeks flushed with the pleasure of coming. Her pussy muscles continued to clench around his cock.

"You feel so damn good," he rasped, loving all the sounds she made, her coos and purrs as he stroked and licked and caressed her. *And every time he smelled a rose, he would think of this night...this moment.*

She was his, and tonight was only the beginning.

He ground his hips against her thighs, his balls slamming against her soft skin as her pussy muscles seemed to suck at his cock. If he hadn't pulled out earlier he would have exploded, and it was all he could do to curb his excitement. Her pleasure came first—would always come first.

He knew the moment she shattered by her sensual moves and the deep, soft sounds that sighed from her throat. Her pussy swelled and gushed more moisture, while the feel, sound, and smell of her finally pulled the trigger on his meltdown.

Jack groaned her name as he thrust into her, hard and reckless like the orgasm blowing through his body.

Pleasure spun him out. Cum spilled from his cock

like a fountain. Finally, the last roll of sensation rocked from his body—his warm, wet, hopelessly spent body—and he collapsed on top of her. When both their breathing patterns calmed, he slipped from her body and discarded the condom before settling down next to her.

"Mmmm...I'd say that went pretty well, Jack."

Jack smiled, plucked his wine glass from the table and levered himself on one elbow to admire her. She opened her eyes, and he thought of rare green gems.

"For the first round. In about five minutes, I'll be hot for you again, Lei," he confessed, and took a sip of his wine.

Keely looked at his cock and gasped. Sure enough, it was ready to go...and so was she! She reached for his wine glass. He laughed and handed it to her, grabbing the bottle of wine to top off the glass before it reached her lips. She took a long sip of the wine before giving it back to him.

"I'm ready for you, too," she said, amazed by her body's response.

"How long has it been since you last had a man?"

She gulped, and reached for the glass again. "Two years."

"How come?"

She shrugged and sipped the wine. "I never wanted to...after my husband, well, now ex-husband," she added quickly when his eyes narrowed, "left me for another woman."

"He was an idiot. Do you have kids?"

She shook her head.

"Would you like to have kids?"

She stared at him. "Y-Yes."

Oh, no-o-o! He couldn't, wouldn't play with her heart, she thought. It was just sex, nothing more.

Jack would be bored, and done, by morning. She was sure of it. Keely counted on it.

"That's good to know," he said, and Keely understood how women's brains turned to spaghetti when he was like this—charming and hinting at a future.

"And you, Jack? When was the last time you were with a woman?" she asked, her skin all goose-bumpy as he caressed her bare hip and thigh.

"About four and a half minutes ago...okay, don't frown. Three weeks ago. I don't like your questions."

Keely swallowed. "What about your...um, previous engagement the other night...?"

"Seeing you that night ruined me for her, I'm afraid," he shrugged.

Keely didn't allow herself to believe what he said, even though the idea of him saying 'no' to a woman gave her a jolt of pleasure. Turned her on, in fact.

"So...how are you?" he asked, his smoky gaze posing the question in a different way: *Can I make you come again?*

She parted her thighs, all too eager to have his magnificent cock sliding in and out of her wet pussy. Her hand closed over his.

"See for yourself," she whispered, and melted for him all over again.

5:00 a.m. the morning after

Jack woke up to the faint sound of early morning waves rippling along on the beach. He shifted on the couch, not wanting to wake Lei, but when he sensed emptiness where her warmth had been, he sat straight up.

"Lei?"

He glanced around and tossed aside the chenille throw that had covered him. The lights from the hotel next door helped him find his clothes, yet not a scrap of hers remained.

He shut the blinds and turned on his desk lamp. The food had been put away, and her roses were gone. No trace of the white-chocolate covered cherries remained—they'd been eaten in very creative ways.

"Get some sleep. We'll go back to my place in a few hours," he'd told her after they'd made love for the third time, "then we'll just spend the day in bed. My bed."

Lei hadn't protested. She did not say no to him or anything he asked of her the whole night long, come to think of it. She would have been crazy to go in to work after being up all night, anyway, so where the hell was she?

He got dressed, brows knotted with concern. Had she made it home safely, if in fact she went home? And where the hell was home, anyway? She was supposed to go home with him!

Fuck.

When he saw her again, they were going to have a little talk. He wanted a relationship, one that included good-bye kisses and maybe a phone number. Amazing concept!

The more he thought about it, the more pissed he got. She had no business leaving him at zero dark thirty in the morning without an escort.

Now, he was going to be sick if he didn't hear from her. As he finished buttoning his shirt, Jack saw the note on the floor. It must have fallen from the table. He picked it up, read it, and swore.

8:15 a.m. Friday morning

Keely couldn't concentrate. Jack just called to say he was on his way in. By the sound of his voice—dark and distant—he was not in the best mood.

Neither was she.

She'd called in sick yesterday, hours after leaving Jack asleep on his couch, a couch they'd shared lust and tenderness. Like when he'd asked her to go back to his place later, like when he'd dropped multiple kisses on the back of her neck, murmured her name, and said "thank you" before dozing off to sleep.

Then there was the note.

Her breath tangled in her throat. To a man like Jack, the words she'd written meant the kiss of death for Lei, but didn't she already know that when she took a pen to the notepad?

The door burst open and Jack strode in. Keely felt her skin singe from the tension radiating from his body. She avoided looking at the cold, hard set to his jaw. "Morning. Any calls?"

"Good morning," Keely mumbled, guilty heat creeping up her face. "The pool builder, Dexter Hu, is waiting for you at the Pandanus Hotel to show you the new pool design. That's it. No other calls."

"Thank you." He stepped into his office and closed the door.

It was going to be a long, dreary day, agonizing over visions of him at his desk, rifling through paperwork, signing invoices, checking his e-mail, and listening to his voice mail.

She committed to memory the sexy timber of his

voice, the way his hand crunched through his hair while he analyzed reports.

She'd made her decision.

No time like the present, she thought, sighing as she picked up the phone and buzzed his extension. "Mr. Sloane, can I have five minutes of your time—"

"No."

"Four minutes, then—"

"No."

"Three and a half…?"

"Keely, you're coming with me," he said abruptly.

"I'm-what?" she asked as he strode out of his office.

"Let's go. If you want to talk, here's your chance. Besides, I could use the company. I'm having a crappy two days."

Oh, great. Her two weeks' notice would go over like a ton of bricks. "Your, um, date with Lei…it didn't go well?"

She knew she had no right to ask and, when his jaw clenched and his blue eyes darkened, she wished she hadn't given in to temptation.

"Nope."

"I'm not dressed to go out," she mumbled, desperate to not be alone with him in public, certainly not in the Pandanus Hotel.

"You're fine as you are."

"Mr. Sloane, I'm dressed too plain to be seen in the Pandanus—"

"Keely, what the hell do you think the Island Lily is—chopped liver?" he snapped. "And right now I want plain. I need plain. Let's go!"

Minutes later they were speeding down Kalakaua

Avenue on their way to one of the island's top-rated hotels. She sat in the passenger seat of Jack's convertible and felt anything but sporty. Her hands fought to keep her bun from flopping apart in the wind. The heat and humidity, combined with her buttoned up sweater, made her feel like she was frying in hell's kitchen.

Even more disconcerting was the fact that the man behind the wheel had been her lover the other night and didn't even know it. She couldn't help remembering his hot, muscled body, and memories of the way his lashes lowered and his blue eyes got all smoky while she licked and sucked his cock forced a guilty lump to her throat.

If he ever found out…

"Ever think of letting your hair down, Keely?" Jack asked as he powered his car through Waikiki traffic.

Her eyeglasses slid down the moisture beading on her nose. Keely pushed them back up with her finger. She shook her head, though she knew very well how to let her hair down.

"You could take your sweater off, assuming you have something decent on underneath…"

She shook her head even harder.

Dexter Hu was waiting for them when they pulled up to the grand entrance of the Pandanus. He stepped forward to open Keely's door while Jack handed his keys over to the valet.

Keely followed a safe distance behind the two men, sneaking a hand up when she thought nobody was looking to undo the top three buttons of her sweater.

The other man led them out to a free-form pool surrounded by boulders and colorful island flora. A series of waterfalls fed into several semi-private grotto-like picnic areas.

She wanted nothing more than to dive into the pool and splash around like the other guests.

Of course, Jack, looking casual and cool in cream cotton slacks and a business casual Aloha Friday shirt with a blue and tan surfboard print drew lusty female gazes. One of them was bound to catch his eye, Keely thought, remembering the woman in the red bikini who'd also gotten better acquainted with Jack in his office.

Keely excused herself to use the ladies room. Once inside, she removed her sweater and splashed cool water on her face. She had bigger problems than being a baked potato.

Leaving Jack Sloane was going to kill her. Rip her heart in two.

But she couldn't stay, knowing he'd move on to someone else, that someday she'd pick up the phone to the sound of his wife's sweet voice on the other end asking for him.

"Well, what a small world, Keely St. John."

The menacing female voice belonged to the biggest nightmare of her life. Keely spun around, gripping the edge of the granite counter for support.

Tayra Lipscomb stared down her perfect nose at Keely. At five feet ten inches tall, Tayra had been a successful island model before she married Rupert Lipscomb, CEO of Lipscomb Hotels.

"I almost didn't recognize you," Tayra sneered. Her cold blue eyes raked down Keely's body. "How the mighty have fallen. Did you hit a yard sale on the way to work, Keely?"

Six months ago, Keely would have trembled under the other woman's icy stare, but for some strange reason, that wasn't happening today.

Keely took a deep breath and, feeling amazingly calm, picked up her sweater. She stood up straight and proud as she shrugged back into it.

"You managed to find work in this hotel after being fired from half the executive hotel offices in Waikiki, eh? Someone finally decide to train you in housekeeping?"

Keely shook her head. "No, Tayra. But that is where I started my career in the hotel industry—in housekeeping. And just for the record," Keely's scornful gaze scraped the other woman up and down, "I can still take out the trash."

Tayra blinked.

"What's the matter, Mrs. Lipscomb? Did you think I'd take one look at you and turn tail and run, like I have been for a year? Three jobs later? How's Rupert, by the way?"

Tayra's curvy mouth quivered with rage. "Don't even say his name, you little slut."

Keely snatched up her glasses. "Tell Rupert I said hi," she said, and started to walk out, but Tayra grabbed her by the collar of her sweater, scraping Keely's neck with her nails.

Keely gasped.

"If you're working here again, consider yourself finished, Keely," Tayra threatened, her face inches from Keely's. "I'll make sure the new manager knows that you screw guests in empty rooms. I'll see you walked out by security like I did once before—"

Keely smacked Tayra's hand away. "Go right

ahead, you lying bitch, and I'll tell my story to the Island Advertiser. The truth, this time! How your husband started spending more and more time at the office to get away from you, and the threats and harassment you put me through. All for nothing! It wasn't me he was having an affair with. I wouldn't touch him with a blowtorch knowing he'd had his dick inside of you at least once—" Keely made herself stop.

Tayra—with her mouth open and eyes bugged out in shock—looked like she was about to stroke out. Keely didn't care. She'd had enough of all the Tayras who hooked up with the good-looking Ruperts and Jacks of this world, then wondered why their men couldn't keep their dicks in their pants!

That will never be me, Keely vowed, stomping past the shocked ex-model. *Ever.*

Chapter Eight

Jack glanced impatiently at his watch. "Where the hell did she go?" he asked Dexter.

"I did not realize she was even gone," Dexter said.

Jack shook his head. Poor plain Keely. So insignificant that even strangers didn't notice her. And then, he saw her, shuffling in their direction, fists at her sides and her head down.

"Anytime you're ready, Mr. Sloane," she said, and Jack's mouth twitched with amusement since he'd been waiting on her in the blazing heat for the past twenty minutes. He said good-bye to Dexter before they left the hotel.

"Are you all right?" Jack asked, and started the car. He noticed her flushed cheeks beneath the heavy glasses and perspiration beading down her neck, at least what could be seen around that God-awful sweater.

She nodded, leaning back in the smoke-black leather seats with her face pointed away from his. "I've just...got a bad headache," she said in a muffled tone.

Jack shook his head and merged into traffic just as the sun crept out from behind the clouds.

He'd be glad once they were back in the office. At least there he could brood in air-conditioned comfort. Not that the couch in his office and its memories gave him any comfort.

He'd like to burn the fucking thing, and even now his fingers itched to burn Lei's letter. It thanked him for a lovely night, the dinner, the roses, the everything else.

It said she wasn't interested in changing jobs at the moment. She didn't feel a need to pursue more than what they'd already shared. It also told him she knew he understood because they were a lot alike, after all.

Nor did the letter leave a phone number where he could reach her to tell her she was wrong.

Not about to discuss anything with Lei's sister, Jack couldn't help but wonder why she spent all night with him if she wasn't interested. A woman didn't do the things she had done unless she was getting something out of it.

Well, multiple orgasms…that and she just really loved sex-like he did. But they shared a lightning chemistry, an emotional attraction that went beyond just one night, or so he thought. He felt used, and he didn't like it.

One way or another, they would meet again.

After negotiating stop and go traffic, they arrived at the hotel's tri-level garage.

He pulled into his shaded stall. "Okay, Keely. Sorry I've been preoccupied, but I'm all ears now. What did you want to talk to me about, hmm…?" he asked, and looked over at her when he didn't get an answer.

"Hey there." Gently he shook her shoulder and noticed tendrils of her hair had teased loose from her bun and now stuck to her neck in wet swirls.

"Mmph," she mumbled. "Thirsty."

Oh, hell no, Jack thought. *She's about to pass out and it's all that fucking sweater's fault!*

He got out of the car, strode round to her side, and opened the door. "If you can't get out and walk, I'm carrying you in," he threatened.

She fanned herself weakly with one hand. "Feel like…I'm about to pass out…"

"Not if you take this miserable thing off!" Jack reached out and yanked her sweater apart, buttons popping and pinging off the dashboard as he did so.

"Jack, n-no—"

He didn't expect to see anything sexy underneath all that scratchy gray wool, least of all the candy-floss pink cotton bustier she wore that cupped a pair of shapely breasts! Jack blinked, glimpsing a smooth, flat waist and tight stomach. She struggled to cover herself.

Too late. He'd seen the body beneath; the caramel-crème skin, the lush curves. His heart banged in his chest as he watched her flounder with her sweater like a dying fish.

Jack scooped her up in his arms, kicked the car door shut, and strode quickly from the parking lot and into the bridge-walk.

Keely slung an arm around his neck and pressed her face next to his collarbone and the pulse that leaped there.

This might be the last time she'd ever be held by Jack Sloane, never mind that his sexy mouth was flattened with annoyance that she would dare to fall apart on him.

She was just glad, so glad to have gotten away from that bitch Tayra Lipscomb before she could carry out on her threats. Only this time, Keely had given her something to think about, and she didn't have to run anymore—except from Jack.

Although, after baking in the sun in her stupid sweater, stockings, and wool-blend skirt, she was no longer feeling so high and mighty.

"I'm sorry, Mr. Sloane," she mumbled as he unlocked the door to their offices.

"You might just be," he muttered, kicking the door aside.

"I'm okay—"

"Shut up."

She said not a word as he stalked into the darkened offices and deposited her on his couch. Seconds later, he handed her a glass of water.

"Sorry," she apologized, wiping at her lips after she slurped the glass empty.

"Feel better now?"

She nodded, and swallowed as memories flooded back of being on this very same couch with him two nights ago. Goosebumps beaded her skin. She scrambled to sit, jerking the flaps of her sweater together.

"I called down to the lobby boutique and asked them to bring something up to replace your sweater," Jack said. The couch cushion dipped as he sat next to her, his hands clasped between his knees.

He studied her clothing, from her crumpled skirt to her drab stockings and the shoes on her feet. In danger of fainting from his hawk-eyed assessment, she stammered, "You didn't have to do that. I-I should get back to work. I've got a lot to catch up on since I was out yesterday."

"Wasn't there something you wanted to tell me, Keely?"

She squinted and pushed her glasses up the bridge

of her nose, looking everywhere but at him. "It can wait."

"Okay. Dinner tonight. You can tell me over dinner."

Over dinner? "I'm b-busy!"

"T-T-Too bad," he mocked. "I realize I've not paid much attention to you these past few months, and I need to fix that."

"You don't need to fix anything. Everything's fine the way it is!"

"I'm not asking you to marry me, Keely," he explained matter-of-factly. "I just want to know you better. Dinner, that's all. So, I want you to take the rest of the day off, go home and freshen up, take a nap—whatever—and I'll pick you up at seven. It'll be my treat for dragging you out today and messing up your bun."

He was teasing her, and she'd nearly suffered heatstroke and a heart-attack thanks to Tayra Lipscomb.

"What about what I want?" Keely asked, a spark of temper flickering inside her. She didn't want to be alone with Jack. She didn't want him paying her—Keely—any attention because then he'd know what—or rather *who*—she was hiding.

"What do you want?" he asked gently.

You, she thought, being unreasonable again. What she should do, she thought irritably, was give him her two weeks' notice. What she said instead was, "I'll call you and meet you in town somewhere."

"Okay, Keely, have it your way."

6:02 p.m.

Jack admired the panoramic view of Diamond Head as the sun descended into the South Pacific. The night lights of Waikiki from the heights of cool, upcountry Makiki reminded him of unstrung pearls scattered down below. He steered his Jag to the curb, two houses away from his destination.

He locked his car and walked toward the cottage tucked along the hillside, under white-blossomed plumeria trees with a killer view of downtown Honolulu.

The property had no driveway, just a column of stone steps accessible from the sidewalk that climbed up to a front yard whose retaining walls spilled over with bougainvillea vines in pink bloom. Jack took the steps, two at a time.

Lights shown brightly inside the house. Someone was home.

He pulled out his cell phone and dialed Keely's number. She answered on the second ring. "It's me. Where're you at?"

"Oh. Hi Mr. Sloane. I'm still at home getting dressed, but I'll be on the bus to town in about fifteen minutes."

"Did the cab get you home safe and sound?" he asked, shoving his hands in his pockets. She did seem a bit relieved to be sent home early.

"Yes, and thanks so much for the T-shirt. I promise I'll pay you back."

"Forget it," he said, thinking about the way the shirt hugged her breasts, how it tapered along her waist before hitting the clumped up waist of her skirt. "Have you recovered from this afternoon?"

"Yes. I showered and took a nice nap."

"So, you're well-rested for whatever the night might bring?"

"Y-you said it was just dinner," she stammered.

"Hmm. Well, we'll just keep an open mind."

"Mr. Sloane, I'm not going to keep an open anything!"

Jack held the phone away from his ear. Interesting, he thought, a bit of emotion showing up in her voice. It was also a very pretty voice when she wasn't forcing it to sound dull and flat. His gaze narrowed and he pressed the phone back to his ear.

"What-what about Lei?"

"What about her?" Jack shrugged. "I can't call her, I can't find her. She obviously doesn't want to see me, so what am I expected to do?"

"So you're just giving up?" she asked in a small voice.

"Gentlemen don't kiss and tell, Keely, but in a nutshell, Lei gave me the best night of my life and then disappeared into thin air. She's done this sort of thing before."

"I don't think so, Mr. Sloane," Keely protested. "She's nice—"

"Yeah? So are con artists," he snapped, cutting her off.

"Umm...where are we eating tonight?"

"Well, there's Dexter Hu's pool-warming party at the Pandanus this evening. We'll need to make a pit-stop there."

He arrived at the top of the landing and saw the kidney shaped pool tucked in the corner of the landscape, surrounded by buttercup-yellow hibiscus hedges for privacy. Mounds of lavender impatiens curved around a small, grassed lounge area where one empty lone chaise sprawled. The front door was carved from koa wood, and in its center hung a funky wreath made of curly twigs.

What a sweet little home, Jack thought. Cozy. Perfect.

He rang the doorbell, and heard an identical sound on her end of the line. "And afterwards we'll go somewhere else to eat. You're more than welcome to pick a place, Keely—"

He paused and heard the sound of footsteps rushing to get the door.

The door swung open to reveal a homely lady in a shapeless mu'u-mu'u, her hair secured in a bun by a set of chopsticks, and those evil, horn-rimmed glasses perched on her nose.

She gasped in surprise, and Jack said coldly, "—or is it *Lei*?"

Chapter Nine

The cordless phone dropped from Keely's hand and clattered to the floor.

Drop-dead handsome Jack stood on the other side of the threshold. He slid his phone from his ear and tucked it into the pocket of his jacket.

I am so busted, Keely thought sickly as he looked her up and down and saw more than her tent-sized dress.

"Aren't you going to invite me in?"

Keely shook her head wildly. "No!" and went to shut the door. If he came in, he'd see everything else, including what was on display on the table in her breakfast nook.

He stuck his shoe out, stopping the door's progress. Keely didn't resist. He was coming in come hell or high-water!

He stepped inside, and his presence filled the room with power and a slow burn of anger as he looked around, before his grim blue gaze rested on her.

She bit her lip, heart pounding in her chest.

"Are you trying to make me crazy?"

"No. Never! Mr. Sloane, I can explain—"

"Damn straight you will! And you can start by losing the Mr. Sloane bit." He swung around, saying nothing as he studied her home, the pictures on the wall, the gallery-class oil paintings in the living room.

He paused at photographs with her in them; her arm slung around the shoulders of family or friends—grinning, laughing—with her brown-gold hair hanging down her bare, sexy shoulders.

"Hmm, no sperm-sterilizing glasses on your face," he observed, moving on into the kitchen. "I don't like being deceived, Keely. I don't like liars, and I don't take kindly to being made a fool of..."

Keely nearly fainted when he spotted the vase of roses he'd given *Lei* and came to a stop at the table holding them. He shook his head, plucked a plum-blue rose from the bunch, brought it to his nose, and sniffed it. "You have some 'splaining to do, Lucy..."

Being put on the spot was killing her, but she had no one else to blame but herself. "I'll explain, Jack, but will you listen?"

"Who's talking? Keely or Lei?"

Smart-ass. She folded her arms across her chest, tamping down her nipples that protruded like little buttons as her senses responded to everything about him. He looked good, and he smelled good.

"I'm listening," he prompted, arching a brow.

She sank against a nearby wall for support. "A year and a half ago, I had a great job managing the Pandanus Hotel. My boss, Rupert Lipscomb, was having an affair, and no one could figure out who the other woman was. Somehow, because I spent a lot of time with him, people thought the other woman was me."

Jack's gaze narrowed. "I know Rupert Lipscomb. Many women find him attractive. Not you?"

"No!" Keely stared at him. "He's married, and he's not my type."

"What is your type?"

Keely gulped, unable to take her eyes off of him—his tousled hair, eyes that hinted at things he'd like to do to her, his hard mouth that could give her the softest kisses.

She cleared her throat and shifted her legs, feeling the friction in her swelling pussy that ached-just *ached*-to feel his cock slip deep inside her. You're my type, she wanted to tell him, but didn't, and simply plotted the ways that she could show him later, if given the chance.

"So then," she said, flushing from the combination of nerves and arousal, "Mrs. Lipscomb spread rumors that I was having sex with guests in their rooms and got me fired. I got another job at another hotel. She found out where I was working, I lasted a week. And so it went until I got this job at the Island Lily."

"Has Mrs. Lipscomb tracked you down yet?"

Keely shook her head. "Since I manage the personnel charts, I can control any information given out about me. And that is where this disguise came in—just in case she asked the staff. How I look now wouldn't fit her description of the way I normally look, Jack."

He pushed his jacket aside and hiked a hand over his hip. His other hand, still clutching the rose, now rested knuckles down on the table. His warm gaze slid along her features. "Like a raving beauty."

She shook her head. "Like a polished professional," she clarified, flattered just the same that he thought of her that way. "I-I just wanted a job where I would be safe from Tayra Lipscomb and her connections; where people didn't smirk in my face. Or try to hit on me because they thought I was easy. I suppose you're going to fire me now, too," she added and fought her bitterness by looking away.

"I just might have to," he said. "Sleeping with your supervisor goes against corporate policy. But right now, I'd like to address some things." He withdrew her note from his pocket.

Keely tensed. Oh no. He couldn't…he wouldn't…

"That is if *Lei* even has the guts to talk to me." His gaze didn't waver.

"I wrote what I believed was true."

He arched a brow and raised the letter, flipping it open with the flick of his wrist. "*Dear Jack,*" he read, "*I didn't want to go without first thanking you for the lovely flowers, the delicious meal, and the very special night that followed…*" he paused to torment her by saying, "I'm glad you thought the night was *special,* Keely."

She shook her head and pleaded. "Why would you be so cruel and read it out loud? I know what I wrote—"

"*With regret,*" he ruthlessly read, "*I must withdraw my job application as well. I'm sure you understand that I couldn't now take a job after last night. While it's been exciting, I have no intention of a repeat performance. I'm glad to have shared a dream night with a man such as you, one who understands sexual attraction and can walk away satisfied without the need to connect with their partner on a deeper level.*"

Oh my God, Keely thought, how could I have written *that?*

"*We're both adults and know how to give and receive pleasure. I hope I've satisfied you as much as you've satisfied me, so I am just going to leave it at that. I wish you well and, should we pass each other on the street, I hope we can greet each other like friends. Sincerely, Lei.*"

His turned-down mouth and stern eyes showed his disapproval. He set the note on the table, next to the rose he'd just set aside as well.

Her turn. She thought she was ready. After all, she'd written the note to serve two purposes—to give him a taste of his own medicine, and to break free of his sexual spell once and for all.

Yet somehow he—Mr. Love 'em and leave 'em— was making her feel really, really bad.

Until he asked, "How long did it take you to write that rubbish, Keely?"

"Rubbish?" Keely stared back at him, her body aching with the memory of leaving him in the early morning hours. How she'd longed to stay wrapped up in his arms. How it pained her to write the words that meant the end of the sensual, short road she'd taken with Jack as *Lei*, and the end of her job—a job she loved but couldn't truly be herself.

Her eyes blurred with frustration behind her glasses as she remembered times when she'd mentally recited all the things she'd love to tell him about his selfish, bratty *self* given the chance, given immunity, of which she had none when it came to him.

But since she was about to give him her two weeks' notice, along with everything else that mattered to her, what could he do? Fire her?

"Rubbish?" she repeated, fighting to tone down the shrill in her voice. "I'll give you rubbish, Jack Sloane! Does it ever bother you that women only want you for your money? Your connections? Your...looks?" she blurted grudgingly before snapping, "Not that you care, since you only ever want one thing from them!"

The silence that followed shattered her ears. She gulped in dismay. But instead of feeling smug and triumphant at the stunned look in Jack's eyes, she felt sick. It wasn't the truth and nothing but the truth, after all.

She'd left out a few bits here and there—like how every inch of her skin still craved his touch, and that her heart's wish was to be the one he wanted for longer than a night or two.

For once in his life, Jack didn't know what to say.

He hadn't counted on hearing how she felt, or what she thought of him.

The reason he came here no longer mattered. The truth in the words she'd just uttered wasn't going away, although he could use the wave of a magic wand right now in dealing with this turmoil.

Jack stared at Keely, seeing clearly now the intelligent sparkle in her eyes beyond her glasses. How could he have been so clueless, not recognizing the curve of her face, her sweet mouth that bloomed so full beneath his kisses?

Had he been so self-absorbed that he'd missed out on her—a real woman—for all these months?

No longer did he just see desirability or loveliness. There was heart and passion there too, coloring the view and forcing him to take a hard look at his attitude toward women. Everything his way with the end result the same.

Not that you care, since you only ever want one thing from them.

What came so easily for him and always got. Sex.

He cleared his throat. "So, let me get this straight. You went through this charade to sleep with me? To get one over on me, somehow?"

"Yes," she croaked. "No."

"Can you be a little more specific?" he prodded, graveness shadowing his voice. He still had his pride. No longer a handy player in this wicked game of hers, he was a man wanting answers.

"You didn't recognize me that night you walked back into the office, Jack. I went along with it, thinking that we'd never meet again. It got out of control, and we wound up having s-sex."

"And that was all you wanted from me? Sex...?" He shook his head. "Dumb question. After all, your game limited you to private, dark-lit spaces and nothing more. Isn't that right?"

"Y-Yes." Her lie sounded clunky and awkward. "It was just sex..."

"Well it was more than just sex to me," he calmly told her through the chaos rioting in his mind. He remembered her limp, near unconscious body in his car earlier that day—and re-lived the shocked instant he knew that his secretary had been his dream lover all along.

"Really? I'd never have guessed, Jack. It's not like I've seen you give any woman in your life cause to think otherwise," she confessed, her chin trembling.

Jack couldn't argue her point, or her perception. She was right. It was true, all of it. But once...

Once, he'd given a woman cause to expect more, much more. It had brought him to a church where he'd waited for his bride to show up. He'd waited and waited.

At least he didn't wait alone. Three hundred wedding guests waited right along with him, as the minutes yawned on with a no-show bride. Jack had faced the inevitable alone, and announced that the wedding was off. He hadn't even had the support of his best man to do the dirty work. His best man had been a no-show, too...

He should just walk away right now with his pride intact, Jack thought, but knew pride would be all he had if he did. That, and his pride wouldn't be worth shit if *Keely* walked away from him. Not that he'd blame her. She'd puzzled him out, teased him, played with his mind, his body.

His heart.

Every male nerve he owned throbbed with temptation to take her in his arms and kiss her senseless, but that would be selfish. The typical brash, bold thing she would expect from him. Not that it would work now on the woman who stood before him—flustered and hurt.

Would she even want more from him now? He wondered, feeling a twisting ache in his gut at the thought that she very well might not. That he might have read her wrong, after all.

He hauled in a breath. No way to find out but to lay it on the line and let *her* choose.

"Keely," he reached out for her hands clenched at her sides. He gathered them in his hands with little resistance.

"Keely, I'm sorry...I have been a complete and total creep. I can't excuse my behavior of the past, but if you let me, I can show you a better man starting right now."

She shook her head, and Jack could see the glint of tears in her eyes behind her glasses. "You have to know, Jack, I'm not one of those women who try to change a man. You need to be you, but I...I need to be me, now. I quit."

Jack exhaled a stunned breath, like his lungs had just been hit from behind. But this was what she wanted.

This was her choice.

"Okay. If that's what makes you happy," he said, his voice soft with sincerity even as his mind fought against the blow.

He lifted her hands to his lips and kissed the back of each one in turn before letting them go.

"May I?" he asked, touching her eyeglass frames.

She nodded, looking a little unsure but she didn't resist when he tugged the glasses from her face.

"Look at me," he gently commanded. She tilted her face up, and Jack smiled into her eyes. No chunky frames obscured the view. He admired her nerve and sass before placing a lingering kiss on her forehead and breathing in her essence for what might be the last time.

"I hope," he said as he drew back, "that you won't feel you need to use these around me anymore." He gave her back her glasses. She stared at them in her trembling hand, then back up at him.

"But for the record, I think you're beautiful either way," he said, and turned to go. He was three steps to the door when she called out his name.

Jack checked his stride, but wouldn't look back.

"Jack, I don't want you to leave."

There. She said it, pushed out the words that pride

had glued stubbornly to her throat. He finally turned to look at her, his blue eyes wary.

Keely pulled the lacquer chopsticks out of her bun. Her hair tumbled down and around her face and shoulders. She approached him, shivering at the dark, sexy look smoldering in his eyes as he watched her.

She stopped in front of him. "I don't want you to go," she blurted through the pain that numbed her heart at the thought of never seeing him again.

She had prepared herself for good-bye, but that didn't mean she wanted it. "I'm sorry, too, Jack. I didn't sleep with you to get one over on you. The truth is…I just wanted one night with you. It wasn't just sex for me. I *loved* every second with you, and I want another night with you-and maybe more after that. That is, if you're not busy?"

His lips quirked with a smile as Keely's face colored with her brazen appeal.

"And allow myself to be used solely for your pleasure?" he asked with irony, since that was the premise she'd just clobbered him with.

"I didn't mean just that—"

"Oh no? Well here's the deal, sweet pea. I'm more than just a pretty face and hot body, so if you want me here…" he pointed to his crotch, making her cheeks burn like a silly school-girl, "…you'd better not be messing with what's here…" he tapped his chest, where his heart beat.

This was why she loved him. Her laugh was choked, yet humbled. "I swear. I won't."

"Will you come with me to the Pandanus' poolside party, Keely?"

"Yes," she nodded. She would walk through fire

for him.

"Tayra Limpsomb might be there, sweetheart," he warned, watching her reaction closely.

The tender way he called her sweetheart made her heart melt with appreciation. "She will and right now I don't care. She organizes these events for Lipscomb Hotels. It's her job as a PR director."

"Are you still afraid of her?"

Keely shook her head. "No. But she is capable of causing a scene, and I'll just have to give her an ass-whooping if she tries to humiliate me." She went on to tell him about her encounter with Tayra earlier, and Jack listened, his eyes narrowing when she showed him the scratch marks on her neck.

"You don't have to worry about her anymore, Keely," he reached for her hand and squeezed it. "I'll be at your side. Always."

She smiled, warmed by the commitment in his words. "Give me five minutes to get dressed."

The poolside party at the Pandanus was packed. A mirrored disco ball and lights glittered down on the dance floor while a band played everything from dance 80s hits to Muse.

Keely tugged at her hem.

After she'd shed her conservative mu'u-mu'u, she put on her sexiest dress; a micro-mini black lace design lined with flesh toned silk that hinted she wore nothing underneath.

She wasn't lying when she told Jack she still wanted him, was wet for him, in fact. She would have let him take her right there in her kitchen, on the table, on the floor, if he'd given her a sign.

But he didn't. He'd behaved like a perfect

gentleman, kept his distance, and waited patiently in her living room while she dressed. But when she emerged from her bedroom in that dress, his mouth parted and his hot gaze said she'd knocked his imagination into full swing.

"Ladies first."

Jack steered her toward the bar where the bartenders were mashing golden cane sugar and fresh mint leaves for the hotel's signature *mojitos.*

They each took a glass. Keely took a long sip of the sweet, fragrant drink.

A busty red-head, who'd been eyeing Jack since they'd arrived, stripped off her cocktail dress in front of him to reveal a black thong bikini underneath.

Keely took another sip of her drink. Oh, this was going to be a long freaking night.

"I guess this means I'm overdressed," she said as the other woman dove into the pool. "I feel sorry for your wife, Jack," Keely chattered on. She could tell him anything now. Why not? She no longer had a fake identity to lose, and it felt so good.

"Why do you say that?"

"She's going to have to put up with this—" Keely waved a hand in the direction of the woman, now floating on her back, her large breasts bobbing like buoys in the water, "—hot babes making a play for you, chasing you, calling you."

"Well, Keely slash Lei," he murmured with an indulgent smile, "my wife would never have to worry. You see, I'm a faithful man when I'm committed."

The thought of him being committed to someone else made Keely fall silent and wish she'd just kept her mouth shut.

"Care for another drink, Keely?" he asked, eyeing her near empty glass.

She nodded.

"I'll be back in a few minutes. Do me a favor and stay out of trouble," he said and winked, making her heart spill over with excitement and pleasure. As Jack walked away, Keely looked around. Any second now that viper, Tayra, would spot her.

Tayra's life mission was to make Keely's world a living hell, but she wasn't afraid. Not tonight. Not anymore.

Chapter Ten

Back at the bar, Jack thanked the bartender, tipped him and, as he was about to leave with drinks in hand, a sultry female voice whispered, "What a small world, Jack."

Preoccupied with thoughts of Keely, he hadn't noticed the sexy blonde slink up to him.

But he recognized the voice and turned to face its owner. "Is it now?" he asked, his gaze sweeping her from head to toe. Everything was still perfect, from her sculpted features to her long neck and playmate body. "Hello, Tayra. You're looking great, as always. How are you?"

Her eyes glittered. "I'm much better after seeing you."

"Really…?" Jack glanced in Keely's direction. She saw them, knew exactly who Jack was talking to and, Jack guessed, didn't know what to do.

Jack turned back to Tayra, aware of Keely's shock, but proceeded anyway.

"Oh come on, Jack. I know you can do way better than that," Tayra added with malice.

"I could," was Jack's lazy response, "but your husband might get mad."

Tayra licked her lips. Jack sipped his drink.

"Rupert's not here tonight," she told him, her

greedy eyes flicking across his face and body appreciatively, letting him know just what she wanted. "He had a previous engagement. Are you here alone?"

"No, he is *not*."

Both he and Tayra looked up. It was Jack's turn to be surprised to find Keely standing in front of them.

"Jack came with me, Tayra, and he is leaving with me," Keely ground out, giving Tayra the fierce look of a tribal princess staking claim on her prince. "So step off!"

Tayra arched a brow. "*You* came with *him*? Oh my. This is just too precious. Keely, Keely, Keely," she tsked, and laughed. "We'll see who leaves with whom. You see, sunshine, Jack and I go back a long way."

Keely could not believe what she was hearing.

Oh, she'd expected to see Tayra here tonight. She'd even expected to be civil when she finally stood up for herself against the beautiful, powerful Tayra Lipscomb.

She hadn't expected the possessiveness that gnawed through her stomach as Tayra talked to Jack— eyeing him like an éclair she couldn't wait to sink her teeth into.

Jack having a history with Tayra was even worse.

Keely looked at them, unable to hide her hurt. She knew that their knowledge of each other included each other's bodies.

Her pained gaze twisted to Jack's calm face. "Is this true?" she whispered.

"Yes," he said.

Keely felt an invisible knife sink into her back.

"After all that I told you," she whispered, and trembled, "you brought me here for this?"

He nodded and said, "This, and one other thing—"

Unable to bear another strike, Keely raised her hand in silent plea to stop him from saying more. Her moment of reckoning had arrived.

Boy, he was good, and she was the stupidest woman on the planet. "No. I don't want to know. You two are perfect for each other—"

"Keely Lei St. John," Jack scolded gently, "is that any way to talk to the man who loves you—your future husband?"

Keely blinked. Oh God, she thought. I've not only created dual personalities, I'm hearing things, too.

"What?" she and Tayra asked at the same time.

Jack took Keely's cold hand, pulled her close, and turned to Tayra, whose eyes sparked with outrage.

"Jack, you can't be serious! You just don't know what you're getting yourself into!"

"I know, and I can't wait, Tayra. I brought Keely here because I knew you'd be here. I knew you'd see me and, just like the last time, you'd hit on me. And," he added coldly, "just like the last time, you'd be turned down flat."

Keely's thoughts spun, watching Tayra's eyes widen at each word Jack uttered with calm, cruel precision.

"I also wanted the pleasure of telling you that if you ever fuck with Keely again, you and Rupert will both live to regret it."

"R-Rupert?" Tayra parroted.

Jack's teeth bared as he repeated the other man's name. "Rupert. My former best friend. My best man. The world's biggest ass."

"What would you have to say to Rupert?" Tayra

demanded, recovering quickly. "I haven't done anything to you—"

"Biggest understatement of the year, *sunshine*," Jack said.

Best friend? Best *man*? Keely wondered what Tayra had done to him, how they'd met, how long they'd known each other, how often they'd had sex, which just made her more mad.

"And make no mistake, Lipscomb Hotels can't handle a stalking and harassment scandal that involves the wife of its CEO. Lipscomb money can't buy you out of that jam, Tayra." Jack squeezed Keely's hand. "Let's go."

Neither looked back as they left the party.

Jack led Keely out to his car and held the door open for her. She got in, avoiding his eyes. He looked dark. Furious.

"Are you okay?" she asked when they were away from the Pandanus, gliding easily in the Jag on the upcountry roads away from Honolulu's city lights.

"Just peachy."

"I don't suppose you'd like to tell me about you and Tayra," she said, choking on the woman's name.

"She's my ex-fiancée."

"What happened?"

"Left me at the altar when she found someone who had more money than I did."

"Rupert Lipscomb?"

Jack nodded.

Keely rested her head back against the seat and closed her eyes. He'd been deceived before, and what she did to him was no better.

His past...it explained so much about him and his

lack of interest in pursuing deeper relationships. "Do you still have feelings for her, Jack?"

"No." The flat, immediate reply reflected his disinterest. At the house, he parked alongside the curb, turned the key, and shut the engine off. The action made her heart skip. Would he want to stay? She turned to him and felt his hunger for her ripple to her very soul.

She sighed, and knew she was going to have to ask.

"Would you like to come up, Jack? I've got nothing to offer-just moonlight and pearls…"

He answered by cupping her chin in his hand and placing a delicious, minty kiss on her lips. "I did promise you dinner, didn't I?"

She smiled into his eyes. "We can start with dessert…"

She led him up the stone steps toward the door to her cottage, but then Jack took control and led her to the pool area, where her chaise-longue sprawled on the tiny lawn.

The tropical night filled the air with soft scents. A pearl-white moon peeked down from high above the coconut trees, and there was nothing she wanted more than to feel Jack deep inside her.

He sat down on the chaise and plopped her in his lap, taking her mouth and kissing her like he had all night. As his hand crawled up her bare thigh, she wriggled in his lap, opening her legs to give him better access to the moistness his fingers sought.

Who was moaning so lustily, she wondered, dazed by the sounds when he swirled his tongue into her yearning mouth.

Her moans turned to gasps as his fingers stroked

her inner thighs, moving higher and higher until he touched her clit. He went still and drew his head back. "Were you panty-less all this time?"

She nodded and blushed, but didn't protest when he threw her back on the cushions, spread her thighs open with his hands, and dove into her pussy.

I'm in heaven, Keely thought, as Jack used his mouth, spreading wildfire throughout her legs and body. Jack seized her clitoris between his teeth and nibbled silkily on the wet petals of her sex. Pleasure throbbed between her legs, but he refused to let up on the raid of her most intimate places, breaking away from her clit to plunge his tongue inside her sheath.

She bit her lip to keep from crying out his name as he gently pinched her clitoris between his thumb and forefinger, launching her into a whole new level of pleasure. He maneuvered his tongue deep inside her cunt to tickle the infamous G-spot.

"J-Jack," she whispered, her mind pulsing with the threat of meltdown into an intense orgasm.

"Hmm?" he murmured against her pussy as he drew out his tongue to lick the juices dripping from her.

He grasped her knees, pressing them up and back so he could enjoy better access.

"I want to come with you inside me," she pleaded, pulling at his big, broad shoulders to bring him up to her.

He shook his head. The tempo of his tongue went from slow and sensual to fast and furious, flicking against her clitoris—side to side, up and down. "Mmm. I want to taste you as you come on my tongue…"

She felt her body tense and coil, about to explode, as she gyrated and thrust her hips against his mouth.

His fingers dug into her knees.

"Jack," she whispered his name, unable to stop herself from plunging as wave after wave of sexual ecstasy crashed through her, flooding her mind and body with pleasure.

When she finally calmed, Jack drew his head back and slid up next to her, pushing her hair back from her face and kissing her cheek, her neck, her mouth. "I'm so sorry I deceived you, Jack."

His fingers undid the zipper of her dress, peeling it down from her braless breasts and tugging it off the rest of her body. He stood up and stared down at her with a half-smile playing over his mouth. He brushed her nipple with his thumb. "I understand why you did it. What I can't figure out is how your hot body snuck under my radar for as long as it did."

Keely laughed, then sighed, her body's pulse points jumping under her skin. She reached out a hand, wanting him again.

Jack's breath caught in his throat at the sight of his woman lounging on the chaise with cat-like satisfaction.

He'd just lapped and licked her to heaven, and the night was just beginning.

She reached out and tugged the zipper of his trousers down. The sensation of her hand reaching inside and caressing his cock threw him off guard.

He'd been both aroused and satisfied pleasuring her, and knew the effect her touch had on him. He was simply mad for her, but tonight was different, and every stroke of her fingertips touched the core of his being.

He held his breath as she pulled his heavy cock out of his pants. Her fingers trembled as she handled him, and she peeked up shyly at him.

"Feels like Christmas," she breathed excitedly and licked her lips.

Jack smiled and smoothed back a curl of her hair that had fallen across her cheek. He groaned as she took his thick member inside her mouth. Her other hand squeezed and jiggled his balls as she sucked his length in deep, inch by inch.

His body hungered for her to ease the ache inside him. Her mouth felt so good, its suction and her tongue worked simultaneously as her hand held him fast, pumping his cock, slickened from her salivating mouth.

"Stop," he groaned, but didn't make a move to push her away. She kept on an on, and finally he pushed gently at her shoulder. "Lay back."

She did, levering the backrest of the chaise down so she could watch him strip off his clothes. Jack fumbled at the catch of his trousers. He couldn't wait to *make love* to her, and she only made things worse when she curved an arm casually behind her head and parted her thighs.

Jack stilled and arched a brow. "Is this night going to get even more interesting than it already is?"

Her smile was that of a pure naughty siren. She slipped her fingers through her perfectly waxed sex lips, parting the wet silky folds for him to admire, stroking her clit in the same motion his tongue had.

Jack watched, fascinated, and listened as her breathing labored. She coo'd his name.

Unable to stand it, he stepped out of his pants and applied a condom as he watched her finger herself. He dragged the rest of his clothes off before joining her on the chaise.

"I have got to have you, so open up, sweetheart," he urged. "This is going to be hard and fast."

"Yes. Oh yes, please," Keely whispered, spreading her thighs to accommodate him as he poised his randy cock at her opening. He thrust into her sex vault, jamming his cock several times into her pussy before she was able to take him to the hilt.

She groaned as he pumped into her, her fingertips digging into his shoulder. "You feel so good, Jack. Just…amazing…"

She trembled beneath him. He flattened his palms on either side of her head and raised himself up. "Will you come for me, sweetheart, while I watch your face in the moonlight?"

She nodded. He drew her hand down to her pussy. Her eyes widened.

"Touch yourself while I fuck you," he whispered, and loved the soft little moans coming from her lips as she stroked her fingers over and around her luscious wet slit while he moved his hips and gunned in and out of her body.

Pleasure. Desire. His body seethed with hot, animal lust. He breached his cock to the hilt in her sweet, tight heat, hell-bent on complete possession of her body, her mind, her everything…

"I love those sounds you make," he growled softly, kissing her ear as she writhed and gasped beneath him.

He'd held back as long as he could, but her scent, her sounds, the way she felt, her creamy cunt and slender thighs wrapped so sexy and snug around him broke the floodgates.

Keely's hips thrust up to meet him. Jack came and came and came, groaning with unabashed pleasure as he lost himself, his mind, his *heart*, inside her slick body

Her pussy milked him of his juices as she came, her walls contracting around him tightly as he surrendered and collapsed in her arms.

They lay there for several minutes, limbs jumbled silkily around each other.

Jack reached up and touched her forehead, her cheek, her skin damp with perspiration.

"I'll never forget this night, Jack," she whispered. "I'll never forget what you did for me tonight. You gave me my identity back, and I won't hold you to anything you said in the heat of the moment."

He frowned, not liking her words. It made him nervous, and he didn't like to feel nervous. He shifted his weight off of her, discarding the condom before turning and cradling her close. "The night's just beginning, Keely."

She nodded, and the movement sent a faint swish of her floral fragrance up to his nose.

"I won't hold you to anything you said to get back at your ex. I know you didn't mean it," she added with obvious distress.

He smiled. "You did look adorably confused once or twice. But I meant what I said."

"Which was what…exactly?" she asked, *sounding* adorably confused. But he knew what she was hinting at, what she wanted to know seemed clear as crystal to him.

"That I am your future husband. I'm just not sure who I want to propose to, yet. Keely or Lei," he teased. "And by the way, you're fired."

"Ohhh…" Keely buried her head in his shoulder,

kissing the skin next to her mouth. Jack felt the love and happiness pour out of her and fill him. "Fucked then fired by the man I love-all in forty-seven minutes. You *so* know how to treat a woman, Jack."

He cupped her breast. "I can't work with you around," he groaned apologetically. "I can't even accept your two weeks' notice. We'd never get anything done. I'll find you a job—"

Keely laughed. "And I'll find your replacement secretary."

He chuckled. "I bet she'll be a sweet young thing, like you."

She gazed at him and smiled. "You don't have to find me a job, Jack. I'm very employable. But I don't want a boss with benefits, just the love of a lifetime."

Jack ravaged her lips with his hungry mouth. "You got it, sweetheart. I want you as my woman and, most of all, I want for you to be the beautiful person that you are, with nothing to hide, nothing to be ashamed of. Ever. Is that okay with you?"

Keely nodded, loving him for caring. Jack's promise of a future melted her. And, he'd given her the best revenge...being loved.

She drowned in his hard male beauty as he lounged back on the chaise—the strong curve of his jaw, his virile shoulders. Her gaze drifted lower, flooding her senses with lust, and love overload. She noted that his cock was already rock-hard and ready to go. He must have seen the hunger in her eyes, known by the way she licked her lips that she wanted all of him again. He handed her a condom and she fit it over his jutting penis, her hands clumsy with excitement.

After sheathing him, she traced her palms up along

his waist, his chest, savoring the warm satin texture of his skin, arranging her body over his until her pussy poised above his full-blown erection. She planted her hands flat on his chest and oh so lazily inched her pussy down his cock.

Jack grabbed her by her shoulders and as his mouth seized, then suckled, on the rosy bud of her breast, Keely whispered, "Anything you want, Mr. Sloane. Anything at all."

All Hands Below

Chapter One

*7 Night Western Caribbean Cruise
aboard the Sea Sapphire*

Day 1

"Are you sure it's safe down here?"

Liam Rossi ducked his head out from under a ventilation shaft as the sultry query floated up to his ears. Stuffing his flashlight into the pocket of his coveralls, he scrambled down the vertical ladder and onto a catwalk in the steamy engine room of the Sea Sapphire.

"It's safe, lovely Evie," came masculine assurance from down below. "And, perhaps the only place I can have two minutes of peace without interruption."

Liam rubbed at the kink lodged in his neck and frowned down at the face of his watch. Ah, yes. It was that time again—the twilight hour. The *courting* hour. He peered at the couple standing in the corridor below.

The woman raised sun-kissed arms and curled them around her companion's neck. Her long throat arched up from an action-packed body whose Christmas-red gown clung to some pretty dangerous curves. Full-sized breasts tanned to a honeyed sheen pillowed up against her companion's uniform dress whites.

When she tilted her face to gaze up at her partner, Liam stared, arrested by the wide-set eyes, delicate sloping cheekbones, strawberry wine lips, and a pert nose.

Beneath a flare of smoky topaz lashes, blue eyes simmered with a look so full of desire Liam suffered a fierce stab of envy for the other man.

"We could go back to your cabin," she offered, her voice lilting hopefully.

"I'm on duty. I should not even be here with you."

"Then come to my cabin later. When you're off duty."

"Not allowed, unless it's official business. But you're here, I'm here and…I'm on fire for you, Evie. I want what's between those legs, sweetheart. Here."

"Now?"

"Yes, now. We could have our own cruise ship mile-high club." Her companion nuzzled her neck. "Where is your sense of adventure, hmm?"

It's not in her pants, genius.

With a sweep of his finger, the other man coaxed one luscious, quivering breast out from behind its velvet slash.

Hot *damn*! Liam smothered a groan. His taste buds puckered and his mouth watered at the sight.

"Look…at…you. Mm-mm-mmm!" The other man breathed and cupped that golden, buoyant mound in his hand.

Concealed in the shadows, Liam watched him squeeze her breast until its pink peak jutted into a pout. The man fingered the wanton nipple to pudgy elongation till it looked like a plug of cotton candy.

Then he guided that tender morsel and its creamy, weighty flesh inside his mouth, deep as it could go, and began sucking.

"Ahh…" The woman's gasp shot a sexual charge down Liam's back, but a frown marred the sweet contour of her lips.

What do you think, sweetheart? Liam mused. *Time to move the party somewhere else?*

She sighed, cupped the man's jaw, and slid a finger inside his mouth to break the rigorous seal his lips had on her tit.

"Evie!" The man protested, pawing at her glistening nipple.

She grabbed her partner's hand and gazed, exasperated, into his face. "Slow down there, speedy."

"Why?"

"Because I want to have some fun with you in a *bed*, that's why. The silk sheets I brought on board are the color of Belgian chocolate. They've never been used." She kissed his fingers.

Liam drank in a pensive breath. Heat sparked from the pit of his stomach and lit into his cock with a sharp, hot singe.

While he struggled to hear what she was saying, his gaze remained fixed on her breast, its rosy innocence rubbing against the officer's dress whites as she pleaded her case.

"Come to me when you're ready, Robert. I want to be with you, but—" she winced. Overwhelmed by the roar of marine diesel engines, she yelled louder, "Not here."

Robert? Chief Security Officer Robert Montero?

Oh *hell* no.

Liam swung out from the shadows and landed on the rubber soles of his boots with a *whump* in front of two startled bodies.

"What the—"

"Officer Montero, how is your wife and baby son these days?"

"Umm…well…"

"Wife?" The rosy flush in Christmas Beauty's cheeks deepened to an indignant red. "Robert, you're *fucking* married? With a *baby*?"

"Evangeline, I—"

"Your presence is needed on the bridge, officer."

"Of course." The other man tripped over his feet, eager to escape the frosty edge in Liam's gaze and hotfoot his way to freedom. "Evie, we will talk later."

"No. We won't."

The other man hurried from the engine room, leaving Liam to wade through a taut silence with the other man's catch of the day. Or night.

"You're in a restricted area, miss," Liam said, no stranger to the party's-over look that crept into her eyes. Her reality ship had just docked, but that usually happened *after* a cruise. This ship had just set sail.

Two engineers came clattering in. She stiffened at the sound of voices drawing near. When he flicked a pointed glance at her breast hanging out in the open, she looked down at herself in dismay.

"Ohh!" Hastily she restored the hill of flesh behind her gown, but the image of her silky hand tucking her breast behind a swatch of red velvet had already branded his memory cells.

The men strolled by. Liam nodded. They nodded back, then gawked at the woman next to him. As one of them ran into a load-bearing pole, Liam guided her away through a maze of machinery and up a ladder, beyond a door, and out of the engine room.

Once inside the safety of an interior corridor, she sighed. "It seems other things were off limits, too." She looked up at him as she removed moldable earplugs.

Misty blue lilacs, Liam thought. As he summed up the color of her eyes, muscles deep in his body throbbed with a blistering awareness of this lethally sexy woman.

He took the earplugs from her and stuffed them in one of his pockets, noting with relief how the baggy cut of his coveralls toned down the ramrod salute of his cock.

"Thanks for what you did back there," she said to him. "You just saved a married man from being naughty, and me from umm…getting…ah…"

"Fucked?"

"Yes. Right. Thanks for sorting that one out for me."

Liam shrugged. "Do yourself a favor and avoid men in dress whites altogether."

She studied the blue coveralls he wore. "Why?"

"Ship's officers meet beautiful women all the time, so you're out of luck if it's roses and forever you're after. Only on a cruise ship do one-night stands last the entire voyage."

Her mouth quirked up. "Thanks for the warning, but I think I can handle a man in or out of uniform."

Liam's gaze narrowed. "Then pick one who isn't wearing a wedding ring."

Her long dark lashes flickered. "Robert wasn't wearing one."

"Funny things rings," Liam drawled. "They slide off at the most convenient times."

"Really? Are you speaking from experience?"

Excitement rioted under Liam's skin. Even his scalp tingled from the challenge that sparkled in her eyes.

He grazed his fingertips down her arm and drifted closer to her, drawn to the floral notes that misted the air around her.

"Maybe."

A blend of spring roses and something else, something fragrant like red, oaky wine, ripened his tongue with anticipation. She would taste as good as she smelled. No doubt about that.

Liam's fingers closed over her hand. He raised it to his mouth and feathered his lips along her silky-soft knuckles. "After all, it does get lonely at sea."

****

Evangeline Spencer gulped as dribbles of *want* soaked through her panties.

Pleasure raced down her thighs and her fingers trembled against the caress of the sexy mouth belonging to this dark-haired stranger. A man who'd stepped in before she and Robert took things too far.

He'd known Robert was married. Yet he risked the wrath of his superior by reminding the other man of his wife and baby waiting at home. This man's actions showed a depth of character that intrigued her. What it meant beyond the next five minutes, who knew?

Evie, proceed with caution! So he has a sex-god face, and a voice that turns your legs to stacked marshmallows, but a heart under the pretty red bow is priority number one.

His mouth glided along her skin, and when her eyes met his, dark and cool like mountain moss, she didn't mistake the glint of humor that flashed in them.

Taking that as a warning flag, she jerked her hand away. It would be a damn shame if he expected some sort of reward for doing the right thing!

"I see." He straightened and arched a sleek brow. "So, you want an officer and a gentleman, hmm? You know the two aren't always one and the same?"

"I don't see an officer or a gentleman anywhere, so I wouldn't know."

He looked down at his coveralls and shot her a wicked smile. "I guess you haven't heard the latest word on engineers. We'll keep your motor running—all night long."

"Hmm, I missed that news flash in my Portland paper. Well, it's been fun but I have to go enjoy the rest of my cruise. Bye-bye."

She turned to leave, but long fingers closing on her upper arm pre-empted her dash to freedom. The touch of his hand on her skin, the hint of cedar in his aftershave mingling with the scent of leather and diesel fuel, made her hot all over!

Her perky nipples must have poked his chest when he drew her against him, too. But by the time he'd employed his stealth-bomber moves on her, it was too late to run. Curling an arm around her waist, he hooked her chin with one lean finger.

"How about a little souvenir to take with you..." he murmured just before his minty mouth covered hers.

I cannot believe this! Evangeline's thoughts raced, but she did nothing to shrug off the wild tingle of his mouth exploring hers. It felt...*amazing*!

Heated fingers swept over the ridge of her spine, rising naked above her gown's bare-back design. It was meant to invite a touch such as this—a caress so teasing yet so potent, her pussy creamed with the hot thrill of it. Sensation melted her will. His soft, skilled lips dove over hers and melted her down.

Coiling her hair around his fingers, he tilted her head to give him better access to her mouth.

As his fingers massaged her scalp, he cradled her head to keep her mouth still, while he fed her the steady pulse of his tongue.

My word, does he know how to wield that muscle.

Suddenly she wanted that tongue everywhere! She burned to feel it lick her nipples, flick at her clitoris, and slide into her silken heat.

Step away from the engineer, Evangeline, was her last thought before she curled into him like a dazed little lamb.

She didn't resist when he grasped one of her hands and glided the tips of her fingers down along the burgeoning ridge of his shaft.

"Hoo," Evangeline exhaled, impressed.

Trouser bulge rising, his cock was shaping up with impressive girth. And length. Quite the humdinger. Oh, yes, indeed!

Shame on me for taking measurements, she scolded herself, then spanned his mighty length with her hand.

Good grief! The man wasn't getting any *shorter.* His brazen words and velvet tongue mimicking the thrusts of a capable cock rubbing inside the grip of her palm let her know he was up for a sexy-hot romp, too.

"Mm-hmm," he murmured and, licking her lower lip, his hands spooned over her ass as he fit her lower body into his like a long-lost puzzle piece.

She plunged her fingers through his rumple of dark hair and imagined his thickness rooted between her thighs. He tugged on the combs that swept her hair up from the sides of her face and dropped them to the floor.

She knew what he'd see; honey-brown hair spilling below her shoulder blades with strands that cooled to golden blonde highlights.

"Take me on, Evie," he invited in a husky voice. "Let me give you what you want."

His breath spiraled in her ear and spilled down her neck. She shivered. "You don't know what I want."

"Officer Montero dry-humping you while sucking on your tit gave me some pretty big clues." The stranger kissed her mouth. Lavished her lips with lusty swirls and tugs of desire meant to chase away any embarrassment she might feel. He lifted his head to assess its rosy response. "Robert's not here, but I am. And, I don't have a wife and kid to make me think twice."

His thumbs brushed her cheeks, and his gaze probed hers with sensual appeal. "Let me be the one to satisfy you. I can even swing the roses."

Evangeline's breath locked on the pull of his words. Not the part where he noticed her being dry-humped while Robert sucked her tit, but every temptation he was offering. Yet, one fine chunk of man candy he might be, there were certain criteria that needed to be met.

"Can you swing the forever part as well? Because I came on this cruise for that, not just some holiday *fucking*. Make no mistake…I want that, too."

His thumbs tensed against her skin. So she didn't pluck the daintiest terms out of the air, but she had no time to dance around the facts. She was on deadline here.

Her heart thumped nervously in her chest. She'd just thrown some heavy words at him, after all. *Forever* and *fucking* were attention grabbers for sure, but had either piqued his interest?

"Questions?" She hoped he had some to ask. She'd tell him the truth—that she'd signed up for this singles' cruise to find a husband. Or at the very least, the start of something beautiful.

Please show me some interest, Mr. Yummy, 'cause then it would be worth it for me to ask your name.

If she scared him off, she'd simply move on and forget about him. Forget the sultry curve of his mouth, his shameless kisses. His bold touch.

A breath hissed past his lips. Decision made, he shook his head, placed a kiss on her forehead, and let her go. No questions asked. "I'm afraid I'll have to pass."

"Thought so." She smiled at him like a good sport. "Will you show me the way out?"

She followed him up a flight of stairs and out through yet another door. He then escorted her to a utility elevator that would take her up to the passenger decks.

"I can help you with one, but not the other," he offered up with an honesty she appreciated, especially given her forward proposal. "But if roses and forever are what you're after…" The elevator doors swished apart. He waved her inside. "Good luck with that."

Evangeline strolled into the lift and turned around

with a smile full of regret. As the doors drifted shut, he touched his finger to his forehead in a nice-meeting-you salute and ended her tour of the engine room.

She brushed a finger against the prickles that danced along her lips.

So this was how it felt to be tempted, tousled, then shot down in flames by a hunky engineer. Nearly getting screwed by one man, then five minutes later slotting *him* in the other man's place. What must he think of her?

And he'd watched them the whole time!

She groaned and rubbed her forehead. Outrageous. Thank God the scruffy devil worked below decks. She need never see him during the cruise. The Sea Sapphire was a big ship. The Western Caribbean was even bigger and would offer wide berth between sightings.

She wanted roses and romance on this cruise, and she wasn't going to apologize to him, or anyone else, for it.

A word about the author...

Just for fun, Lelani Black used to write motocross articles for a motocross website. One day a sports editor for a national magazine read one of her articles and invited her to submit her articles to them—for money! That one kindness shown to her by an editor gave her the confidence to keep nurturing her passion for writing. Her debut erotic romance, Boss With Benefits, was her first foray into her journey as an author of erotic, romantic fiction. It's been full-throttle fun ever since!

www.ingramcontent.com/pod-product-compliance
Lightning Source LLC
Chambersburg PA
CBHW071405170626
46811CB00003B/1271